£16·95

D1433612

IN AND OUT OF THE FOREST

Also available in this series:

IN AND OUT OF THE FOREST

Winifred Foley

ISIS
LARGE PRINT
Oxford and Orlando

Copyright © Winifred Foley 1992

First published in Great Britain 1984
by Century Press
Revised edition published by Thornhill Press Ltd., 1992

Published in Large Print 1998 by ISIS Publishing Ltd,
7 Centremead, Osney Mead, Oxford OX2 0ES,
by arrangement with Winifred Foley c/o Christopher Foley

British Library Cataloguing in Publication Data
Foley, Winifred
In and out of the forest. – Large print ed. – (Reminiscence
series)
1. Foley, Winifred 2. Country life – England – Dean, Forest of
3. Large type books 4. Dean, Forest of (England) – Social life
and customs – 20th century
I. Title
942.4'13'085'092

Printed and bound by MPG Books Ltd, Bodmin, Cornwall

Dedication

To my husband and children

CONTENTS

CHAPTER
ONE

It is Christmas Eve, and just on cue the first snowflakes of winter have begun to fall. Soon they form a mist obliterating the view from my window. I can no longer look out day-dreaming of what the future holds. Never mind, I pull my chair up nearer to the fire, add some fresh lumps of coal, and chew over the cud of past memories to help enrich the hours until taken to "that bourne from which no traveller returns."

"I remember, I remember, the house where I was born," wrote Robert Browning, and I remember, too. Growing legs long enough to get over the board placed across the doorway to keep me in. Trying to pull a blue flower off the periwinkle that smothered the dividing wall between Granny's tiny courtyard and ours. The struggling progress to the top of the steps and into the garden from which vantage point I could get my bearings. The latch of the garden gate was high out of reach. Never mind, there was the garden world to explore. Down the path I went between the candytuft and the sweet williams, staring with astonishment at the size of the red paeony blossoms on the corner where the middle path took off, but not liking their smell when I pushed my nose into their fat faces. My sniffs were more disdainful as I toddled past our bucket privy, despite its covering of honeysuckle. I made quite a pause to admire the roses climbing over the rustic arch down the middle of the path. Dad had made it from windfalls in the Forest.

Dad was not there, so there was no need to go down to his little wooden workshop hut where he mended our boots, patched up pit-lamps, and put back together broken and worn-out furniture for us and his neighbours; all for goodwill and because he had the skill to do it. The branches of the plum tree were well out of reach, but not for the lucky little brown bird I spotted in its branches. Later on, when the plums were ripe I called up to it "Little birdie, little birdie, please throw me down a plum", but alas it took no notice of me. Then up I toiled between the potato haulms to Dad's beehives, where I settled down right in front of one to watch the busy comings and goings of the bees, unperturbed by those that flew around my head, until suddenly I was grabbed by Mam.

"The little varmint", she cried to Granny, "got outside somehow whilst I was scrubbin' out the back-kitchen. 'Er could've bin stung to death!"

But the stings and arrows of outrageous fortune were still to come; just now loving arms, and innocence still unpolluted cushioned danger. It is no wonder we old ones love to remember such times.

Sometimes I feel that I was born in a little stone cubbyhole in one of Nature's beautiful palaces. It was royally owned for it was Crown Property — the Royal Forest of Dean in Gloucestershire. I came into the world in late July 1914; on a feather-bed on an iron bedstead, covered with a patchwork quilt in a tiny cottage bed-room. And nodding me a welcome against the window panes were the roses, one dawn-pink and one velvety-red, that climbed the wall each side of the cottage door. My first walk in Mother's arms along the forest path outside our garden gate, was a setting fit for a princess, with tall trumpets of purple foxgloves growing profusely among lush green ferns dappled with sunlight coming through the branches of magnificent oaks. No princess I; just a plebeian scrap of humanity of no more signifi-cance in this lovely habitat than a scurrying beetle in Buckingham Palace.

My "Palace" was surrounded by a winding moat formed by two rivers: Severn and Wye. Its enclaves were pillared with ancient oaks and its corridors carpeted with green grass kept mown by the wandering sheep. Nature, the greatest artist of them all, changed the decor with the seasons. In winter the heavens laid their shampoo of snow to be rinsed away by sprinklers from the clouds, and it was quiet in the woods, for most of the resident orchestra had flown away to spend a holiday in warmer climes. We lived in a gallery of etchings with the delicate black tracery of bare branches against the white floor and the ceiling of pale grey clouds.

Then the magic! The sky changed to pale blue and fluffy white, and the spring buds misted the trees in delicate green. Like fairy umbrellas, myriads of fern fronds poked their way through the earth, keeping neatly to their territory with the foxgloves under the trees, and leaving the bluebells to stake their claim nearby.

Everything stirred again; the fauna in the undergrowth, the squirrels in the trees. Out came the garden spades, and the sharp winds of Spring whipped us all back to energy, while the winter bedclothes that could now be washed danced on the line. "Put, put, put egg", the hens began to squawk, and truant ones emerged from beds of nettles with families of fluffy chicks.

Summer slowed us all up a bit. Nail-booted, weary miners caked in pit-dirt plodded up our hill to home. Between their flurries of black-leading their grates, carrying out the buckets of ashes, scrubbing flag-stone floors, wielding the heavy dollies in their washtubs, and minding their little ones, the housewives found time to sit awhile on the grassy banks outside their cottage gates to gossip. We girls made cool havens in the ferns for our make-believe games of shops and houses, with the lucky ones bringing out their dolls to be doted upon. The livelier boys went their own way, a-Tarzanning it among the trees, or stripping off to plunge in the streams they dammed up to make little pools.

Daylight hours were shorter, to spend in the tawny golds of Autumn. Then boys and girls together descended like locusts on any edible bounty of nature we could find, blackberries, nuts, ripe hawthorn berries, and illicit raids on the rare apple tree or pear tree out of sight of a window.

But palaces can have their murky corners, and their dungeons too, and here the coal-cellars were deep under the earth. The rights to these fuel stores had been obtained by a few rich men. These coal-owners employed most of our male inhabitants, young and old, to go down deep shafts in cages to burrow like animals, often on their knees or stomachs, to pickaxe this rich black relation of the highland peat pressed into seams of earth's black diamonds over millions of years by the weight above them. Many of the men and boy workers were killed or injured at this dangerous task, for which they were not paid enough to keep the bodies and souls of their families together. There were few crumbs then available to them from the rich man's table.

Less than a century ago little boys of ten or younger followed their fathers down the pit as hob-boys, as my own father did at the age of eleven. A chain round his waist and between his legs was attached to a sled, and so he dragged the coal that his step-father had pick-axed out to the bottom of the shaft. It was rare indeed that they worked in a place high enough to stand in. Occasionally there were areas round the base of the shaft high enough to use pitponies — creatures that lived, and were often born, under the ground. When they were too weak or too old for work and were brought to the surface, their underground life had made them blind.

The meagre earnings of sons and fathers were too perilously stretched to feed sisters and daughters, and little girls could not go down the mines. So, capped and aproned, they must be reluctantly parted from to wait on the tables of the affluent, and to carry up from their own dungeon-kitchens the coal hewn out by their menfolk to stoke the fires in the luxurious upstairs quarters. School had become compulsory to fourteen years old by the time that it was my turn to leave my family and my beloved Forest of Dean. Unless we eventually returned to marry a miner ourselves, we knew it was good-bye forever except for the respite of our annual two weeks' holiday.

How great must have been the pleasure of the miner when he stepped from the cage at the end of his shift, and out into the glory of his surroundings. The character of the Forest miner was moulded by the sharp contrast of his life above and below ground. In summer he walked to the pithead through a sunlit sylvan paradise; then, down the pitshaft to crawl like a primitive animal hacking out the coal for a society which generally regarded him as little different from a dirt-grimed animal. It turned some men bitter, and some into visionaries; some, like my father, were both.

And what a dip back into our Elysian childhood was our fortnight's freedom from the almost total incarceration of basement and attic! In service, our bellies were mostly filled as they could never be at home, but there was an empty ache in many of our hearts. Nowadays I get many letters from Forest girls. They come from all over Britain, from Canada, America and Australia. In old age many now enjoy an affluence undreamed of in our childhood days. But through all the letters runs a nostalgia for those far-off days in the lovely Forest of Dean.

Dotted strategically about were some grander stone cubby-holes, the chapels; and a few even grander and larger and more ancient, the churches. In these on Sundays many of the inhabitants gathered to sing their thanks to our unseen benefactor for all His blessings, and to ask Him to forgive us our trespasses and lead us

6

further out of temptation. We never figured out what blessings our parents were so thankful for! It was different for us children. We had the chapel summer treat and the annual outing to be grateful for, and a blind eye from above on our trespasses for stolen plums and apples. It was always the villagers who caught us, and they administered chastisement at once, on our behinds.

An old chap in our village was digging up a fine crop of potatoes for winter store, when a fervent local preacher looked over the garden wall, and piously reminded him to be extra thankful in his prayers that night. "Oh, aye?" demanded the old man, "and who shall I thank for all they bloody caterpillars that's ruined all me broccoli and cabbage plants? An' them dattlin' blackfly that took all me broad beans in the spring?"

CHAPTER
TWO

Without such things as radios, televisions, and phones, and with a car being a rare sight the folk of our village, though well aware of the big wide world outside the Forest, were not unduly curious about it. And from what they read in the *News of the World* they did not hold too high an opinion of it. So it was considered a novel and daring idea when some bright young spark among the habituées of the village inn put up the idea of a pub outing to London. They chewed the matter over with their cuds of twist tobacco, and gulped the notion down with their ale, and eventually agreed; yes it was a fine idea.

Even Bodger said aye. Bodger had been born late to his highly respectable chapel-going parents and he must have been a great disappointment to them. As a young man he had "took to the cider", and getting as much of it as possible down his gullet became his purpose in life. After he had paid his mother her modest demand for his board and lodging, as one crude commentator put it, "He pissed the rest of his wages up against the wall." He never really got the worse for drink — he had nowhere to store it; he was so thin and tall he had begun to droop from the shoulders. But neither was he very properly sober.

Now they had the idea for the trip the problem was who was going to organise it for them? There was a big-wig in the village, the man who owned the local stone quarry. He employed four men, he knew about business matters, and he had been to London several times. A couple of delegates were chosen to approach him on the matter. Being a man of business he gave it some thought and agreed, providing that his own expense for the fare and the meal he would organise for them in London came out of their funds. He would also act as guide to show them some of the sights of London. Fair enough, they agreed. The quarry-owner worked out the cost; the return train fare and half-a-crown per head for the cooked lunch at the Great Western Hotel at Paddington. What pocket-money they took was their own affair.

The landlady of the inn took sourly to the idea; her takings, little enough at the best, were appreciably lower for the month they were saving up. Bodger's weekly payment was extracted from him on pay night before he ordered his first glass of cider.

Eventually the great day dawned. Wives and mothers were up early to see their men off; best navy serge suits, reserved for funerals, were brushed and pressed and sponged; freshly-washed white mufflers, borrowed if need be; and black boots polished till you could see your face in them. Unselfish wives, determined that their husbands should not look poverty-stricken in the great city, gave them the money put by for the tallyman, the insurance man, and the grocery bill. With money to rattle in their pockets, filled with the spirit of adventure, they set out to walk the mile through the woods to the little halt where they would board the train.

Including the organisers there were thirteen of them, a fact which caused some consternation.

"Thirteen be an unlucky number." "We bain't thirteen, we be twelve. We don't a' to count Mr Tyson in. 'Im's a somebody; 'im's bain't one of us."

"'Im's a man the same as us lot. We 'a' got to count 'im in. Let's drop Bodger." (Bodger was out behind the pub at the time making room for more cider.) Eventually the spirit of democracy prevailed and now Bodger strode happily along with the others. For the umpteenth time the organiser stressed that if by any unlucky chance they got separated in the crowds anyone lost must find the nearest policeman and explain what had happened and then get back to Paddington Station.

With an air of unfamiliar importance they settled back into the luxury of the plush upholstered train seats and marvelled at the unexpected size of England as the train chugged interminably on. And bewildered as a truck load of sheep brought from the fields to market they found it difficult to appear nonchalant among the busy comings and goings of trains and people when they stepped out on the platform at Paddington. They marvelled at Mr Tyson. He was not at all overwhelmed as he shepherded them out of their exit and into the grand entrance of the Great Western Hotel.

They pushed their pit-scarred hands into their pockets as they were shown into a huge dining room where all the white napery and the abundance of cutlery and cruets made one whisper to another; "I do feel like a fish out o' wayter in 'ere."

"Aye, but let's kip a' eye on Mr Tyson and do the same as 'im." Anyway, they did know what knives and forks and spoons were for, and the way to their mouths, and if the food went down a little slower than usual and if a few beads of sweat came out on a few foreheads in case a drop of gravy soiled a tablecloth, they had after all paid for it.

The waiters cleared the plates away. "Ow much was that lot, then?" asked Bodger of the waiter at their table.

"Half a crown, this luncheon, sir."

Half a crown! Back home he could have had a gallon and a half of cider for the price of that meal, thought Bodger ruefully.

"'Ere you be then," he said, and he handed the waiter half a crown, and was surprised and mollified by the way the waiter bowed low saying. "Thank you. Thank you very much, sir. I hope you've enjoyed your meal and will come again sir."

As they made their way out into the street Bodger asked the others, "Did you see the way thic waiter bowed and scraped to I when I paid 'n the 'alf-crown for me dinner?"

"What's mean; paid 'n for thee dinner? All our dinners was paid for by Mr Tyson. Thic 'alf-crown came out o' what thee'st been payin' 'im every week!"

Bodger was stricken by his terrible mistake. All that cider money thrown away? Never!

"I didn't know. I must a' been out the pub-back when

all that was said. Well I'll tell you what; I don't care if thic waiter 'ad bowed an' scraped till 'is 'arse touched the ceilin'. I be going back in an' askin' for me 'alf-crown back!"

"Thee coosn't do that, Bodge. Thic waiter thought thee'st tipped 'n 'alf a crown," and they had to force him physically on up Praed Street. But comfort was soon at hand for Bodger when they came to the pub, The Load of Hay. "I be a-goin' in 'ere for a drop o' cider", he announced resolutely.

"Oh, come on, Bodge. We bain't come to London for that, we do want to see the sights."

They all took a firm stand against the idea, but keeping Bodger out of a pub was like trying to keep a pin away from a powerful magnet.

"We can't drag the drunken bugger all round London. Let's leave 'im 'ere an' pick 'im up on the way back." There was no option anyway; Bodger had gone inside.

Buckingham Palace was a solid-enough looking place but nothing like as pretty as they had imagined and one observed he would rather get his living down the pit than marching up and down "like a toy clockwork soldier wi' a gret fur tea-cosy on 'is yud".

The Houses of Parliament, London Bridge, Trafalgar Square and Piccadilly Circus came in for their meed of praise and criticism. The cup of tea they had in a café was no better than gnat's piddle, and the price of the little fancy cake was daylight robbery. But the shops were something different, and soon their pockets were bulging with cheap brooches, necklaces and toys for their families. And all concerned had been most impressed by Mr Tyson's ability to get them around the maze of streets and in and out of the traffic, buses and trams.

All in all it had been a wonderful day. London was certainly a remarkable place, even if the people who chose to live there must be a lot of lunatics. They were not sorry to be walking back down Praed Street to the train that would carry them back to the Forest. They got to the Load of Hay at closing time, just as Bodger and a few reluctant customers were being turned out — a disconsolate Bodger, for as usual his money had run out before his thirst.

"Come on, men, step it out, the train's due any time now." Mr Tyson got them onto the right platform and then counted his flock. "Where's Matt? Where's young Matt? He isn't here." The distraction of London had been all too much; they had not even noticed that Matt was missing.

"'Im was wi' us when we was at Piccadilly Circus. I be sure o' that, 'cos 'im was sayin' 'im didn't think much o' thic statue there that 'is teacher 'ad told 'em about at school."

"That was hours ago," moaned Mr Tyson. "If he got parted from us then, he should have got directions from a policeman to Paddington and been there by now. Oh dear, I hope he hasn't got into any sort of trouble."

"Don't worry about Matt, Mr Tyson, 'im's a big strong lad, 'im can take care of 'isself, 'im's a match for any Londoner. Besides 'im bain't short of a bob or two, bein' a single man. I know for a fact he brought a good sum o' money wi' 'im so 'im'll 'ave to buy 'isself another train ticket."

"Oh my goodness, here's the train. We shall have to get on it. I'll contact the police first thing in the morning. But what shall I tell his parents? The young fool, he's spoilt the day. I wonder wherever he can be?"

Eros must have taken Matt's snub to his heart because he sent a mischievous messenger to waylay him with a pair of inviting eyes in a painted face atop a tight skirt, high-heeled shoes and a provocative walk. Matt followed the age-old path, down twisting streets to a tall house and a room among the chimney pots. He emerged with only the lining in his pockets, but he did not feel robbed. He returned home the following day a wiser but not a sadder man.

His mother was amazed to hear that the pickpockets of London were so clever that they could take the money out of a man's trouser pockets without his feeling a thing.

Matt did not share Bodger's sentiments. When the party stopped at Gloucester station to change trains for the little halt, Mr Tyson got into conversation with the assistant station master to discuss the problem of the missing Matt.

Bodger was not intimidated by the resplendently uniformed figure of railway authority, and told him, "You can take your rails up now, guv'nor, for I shan't want to be goin' up there again."

The women never went into the pub. That would have been disgraceful; so would smoking, or giving vent to their frustrations in the kind of language the men used — although there were some who had been known to use

14

the milder expletives. The football and quoit games were also exclusively male territory. Only chapel-going, and the dull domestic routines in the orbit of the hearth, were the lot of women. Anything other was unthinkable, until one day the spirit of Women's Lib, in the strident voice of Edie, roused them out of their apathy.

"Why," she demanded, "should the men have an outing, and not we?" There really was no answer to that, and Edie drove the point home. Of course they would not do anything silly like going to London, where pickpockets roamed the streets, and where they might lose a child in the crowds; for of course they would be taking the children to give them a treat too. What Edie had in mind was a trip to the seaside, to Barry Island. They could hire a charabanc for a Sunday in the summer. Let the husbands feed the pigs and the chickens and get their own victuals for a day! It would do them good!

As well as the small core of enthusiasts, the timid and the doubtful were soon persuaded by Edie to join the scheme. Especially when Mrs Jupp, who took the children's weekly teetotaller's class, accepted the role of treasurer. Edie would arrange the outing for August, so they had months to save their pennies for the great event.

Husbands varied in their response to the idea. Not all of them were pub-goers or had been to the men's outing. Some were quite willing and those that were not were soon overruled by their newly militant wives.

The day of the outing promised to be a real scorcher; just the day for a trip to the seaside. Down they trooped, old women, young women and the children to the charabanc at the bottom of the village. Alas, many of the children, full of excited anticipation, handed round sweets, and the shock of the unfamiliar ride in the charabanc made them sick. The driver had to make many stops by the roadside, but this was all soon forgotten when they got on the beach.

Women and children hitched up their skirts and went for paddles. "Oh Gawd! My veet 'ave never 'ad such a good soak 'afore!" sighed Edie's old mother contentedly as she sank down on the sands. The long hours of sitting in the sun tempered by the sea breeze, doing nothing all day — the women all agreed it was just the tonic they needed. Refreshed in mind and body, and full of good humour, when the driver called them for the return journey, they shepherded their offspring on to the charabanc. He had to make several stops on the way home too. The children who had not been sick on the way down made up for it on the way back. Some were overtired and fractious and some had caught the sun badly.

Well, it had been a grand outing but it would be a relief to get back to the village, where no doubt husbands and fathers would be anxiously waiting to carry the sleeping children home to bed. And probably a little bit of fire in the grate with the kettle singing on the hob and the cups on the table!

The noise of the battle was not yet over when the charabanc drew up in front of the courtyard of the pub. Casualties were all over the place. Some leaned up against the walls, and some were still in combat. Like a classroom of repressed boys when the teacher had been called away with the women out of the way, masculine aggression had had a field day. Irritated by outlandish domestic duties, and with their bellies inadequately catered for, they took their seething discontent to find solace in the pub.

A small self-contained village is a stewpot of personalities much influenced by the dependent gentler sex and by the needs of the children. The women wielded the wooden spoon that kept the pot from boiling over and leavened the aggression of the men by the love, respect and tolerance due to them. One whole day without the women's restraining influence had been too much.

It had all started with a little argument between two men about an old grudge from the time when they had worked as butties on the same coal seam. Sides were taken and a fight broke out among the participants. The elderly landlady, who had never before experienced this sort of trouble, had managed to clear the pub and lock the doors before too many chairs were tipped over and too many glasses broken. Soon the fights became a mêlée, little factions breaking off to fight among themselves, some for the sheer hell of it and others to exorcise jealousies, old scores, and grudges past and present.

The bewildered women stood aghast at the spectacle, the pluckier ones crying "shame on you" as they struggled to part those still in combat.

"It's like a bloody battlefield," cried Edie. "Can't leave the great gawbees alone for five minutes 'afore they turn into a lot o' wild animals." She found her own husband lying supine by the wall; concussion or over-indulgence in cider, she neither knew nor cared. Unlike the others she offered no ministrations or help to get her battered spouse home.

"'Im can lay there till Christmas an' get icicles on 'is arse for all I care," she said.

One teetotal husband was sitting peevishly indoors.

"Oh, you be 'ome at last then, I a' bin waiting all day for thee to make me a cup of tea," he greeted his wife. And then he got the surprise of his life.

"Oh, 'ast thee?" and she took him by the scruff of the neck to the pan of drinking water in the back kitchen.

"Look, that's water. You puts it in the kettle, you know that thing that sits on the 'ob wi' a 'andle and a spout — when it comes to the bile you take down the tea-caddy. That's the tea-caddy, thic tin on the mantlepiece that a' bin there these ten year we a' bin married. Then you puts two spoonfuls in the teapot. That's thic thing I 'a' bin pourin' thy tea out of these last ten years. Fill it up wi' the bilin' water out o' the kettle an' thee'st got theeself a cup o' tea. And now I could do wi' one, so thee set to an' make it!"

And he did!

The shock waves reverberated around the village for quite a while. Eventually harmony in the pub and on the home front was established again, but going out into the world had broadened many an outlook.

CHAPTER
THREE

Soon such indulgences as outings became unthinkable. Life became a grim struggle to survive. The mining communities of England began to slip even further into the post-war recession, as the government took the coal from Germany as reparations for war debts. Hours of work were drastically reduced, and then the mine-owners demanded a wage-cut from seven shillings a shift to six. The men, already losing the battle to feed their families, and knowing that the mine-owners had made rich pickings during the war, turned their despair to anger and went on strike. One of its victims was my Auntie Lois.

One of the bonuses of my early childhood was the fact that Granny and Grancher lived in the cottage next door with their young son Stan, and his bevy of older sisters:- Olive, Winnie, Gladys, Beatty, Lois and Phyllis. Elsie, who was between Beatty and Lois, had come home from her job in service to die of consumption, an all too common complaint in the village. Earlier, Olive, who had married a young miner, escaped the slough of economic despond that the Forest mining area was becoming. Her husband inherited two cottages from an uncle, and he sold them to sail steerage to America. He found a mining job in Illinois, and sent the money for his wife and six-week-old baby daughter to follow him.

My other aunties were all away, in domestic service. They were good girls; out of their few shillings a week wages they bought their clothes, saved up for coming home on their annual fortnight's holiday, and brought home all they could get hold of to share around; packets of twist tobacco for Grancher, treats for their little brother, anything for us to wear that had been thrown out in their jobs, and some extra shillings for Granny's housekeeping. Some of their bounty was shared with our Mam for her three children.

I loved them all, but Aunt Lois was my favourite. Grancher regarded his daughters as an amiable, more or less harmless, bunch of lunatics. He sat in his special wooden armchair by the fire like a dour old bumblebee while these dainty butterflies he had begot prepared themselves in their finery to go to the local dances when they were on their holidays.

Grancher only knew of two sorts of material for women's clothes — flannel and muslin. Like her sister Elsie, Phyll the youngest daughter was plagued with a chesty cough. Once, on her holidays, she got ready to go to a dance. Alarmed at the brevity of her diaphanous thin dress, Grancher actually went to the door and shouted to Granny, who was in our cottage "Liz, Liz, thee come on in 'ere an' look at our Phyll. 'Er 'a changed out of 'er flabbels, an' into 'er muzzels, an' 'er'll catch 'er dyuth o' cold goin' out like that."

It was at such a dance in her holidays that Auntie Lois attracted the admiration of a fine handsome young miner from a nearby village. The attraction was mutual, and for the rest of her holiday, when he was not down the pit he was waiting under the trees on the bank outside Grancher's garden gate. He worked in the same pit as Grancher and could not summon the nerve to come to the door. He did not know, as we did, that Grancher was all growl but no bite. It was my job to go up to the gate to see if he was there; for doing which I felt amply rewarded by a dab of powder on my snub nose from a leaf of Auntie Lois's dainty papier-poudre book. In feminine fashion she always kept him waiting, but their eagerness for each other's company was so great that Auntie Lois looked the picture of misery when her holiday was over.

Courting by letter is a poor substitute. Lois was lucky. that her mistress was so pleased with her that she allowed her a week's holiday twice a year instead of the usual annual fortnight. Absence must have made their hearts grow fonder. A year later they could stand the separation no longer, and decided to get married. What chance has commonsense, when Nature uses Cupid to gain her ends? They well knew it meant setting up home in any humble cottage they could rent, and living on a shoestring budget, but it was better than the heartache of separation.

I used to love to go and see Auntie Lois. The aura of her happiness, and the neat cleanliness of her home, more than made up for the sparseness of the furnishings. And poor as they were she always found something to fill my belly. When a baby boy came along they seemed happier than ever with each other, and their joy and pride in the baby was boundless.

But the depression in the coalfields now made things very difficult. I still remember my childish misery and embarrassment when Auntie Lois burst into tears because she could only spare me one piece of bread and a scrape of jam to eat. Desperation turned to real hopelessness when the strike began. Lois and her young husband were prepared to put up with the limits of hunger themselves, but she had enough sense and experience to know the effect of malnutrition on children. My own younger brother and sister both had spells in a sanatorium. Lois could not bear her beautiful year-old baby to be underfed. Only a loving devoted young mother can appreciate the decision Aunt Lois now had to make. To feed her son she must part from him, and go back to domestic service. She must sacrifice her wifehood as well, to earn her baby's keep until the strike was over. Rightly she anticipated that Granny would take the little boy to live with her, a task that child-loving Granny would regard as a privilege; though she wept bitterly that her daughter was brought to such a pass.

So Aunt Lois wrote to her former mistress for a reference, and explained why she needed a job. She got an immediate reply. Her mistress had a friend, an elderly widow of a rector, who needed a companion-housekeeper, and she had highly recommended Lois. The rector's widow would be writing offering a wage of ten shillings a week and travelling expenses.

It was anguish for Uncle Bill not to be able to support his wife and child, and now having to live apart. Only bereavement could have made them more miserable when she kissed him and her baby good-bye at the little railway halt.

"A treasure" was a word commonly used by a mistress for a good servant, and the rector's widow had never known such a treasure as Aunt Lois. A sad young woman, true, but what a willing worker! Never wanted to go out, not even on her half-day off, domestically skilled, able with her needle, quite intelligent to converse with, and the only favour she ever asked was to be paid weekly instead of the usual monthly. The weekly postal order of nearly the whole of her ten shillings sent to Granny, was the beacon that brought a ray of hope into Lois's lonely life. The ache to hold her baby was unbearable. To work until she was tired out, to keep busy so there was less time to brood, helped her through each day, but every night she cried into her lonely pillow.

Granny's heart was aching too. She understood how Lois must feel. She could not read so Grancher had to read out Lois's letters to her, and even he had to pause and clear his throat and wipe his eyes. He, too, was now out on strike, but Phyll, Winnie and Gladys sometimes sent a postal order for a couple of shillings. So Granny managed, after three months, to scrape enough together for Uncle Bill to take the baby to see his mother. "We won't tell 'er", she said, "we'll give the wench a lovely surprise."

It was the habit of Lois's mistress to rest on her bed every afternoon, and on no account was she to be disturbed. Lois was busy in the kitchen, doing a pile of ironing, when the knock came on the back door. Her surprise and joy at the sight of her baby in Uncle Bill's arms nearly made her faint. But her heart almost broke again, when the little boy did not know her, and clung to his daddy away from the "stranger". Poor Lois! How it broke her spirit and her resolution! "I be comin' 'ome wi' you," she sobbed, "I can't bear it any longer," when at length the baby submitted to being cuddled on her lap. "I be goin' to wake Mrs Havers up, an' tell 'er I be leavin' now."

When a rather irate mistress bade Lois to come in she was soon wide awake as Lois sobbed out her dilemma, and said she would never be parted from her baby again. "Pull yourself together, Lois dear; go back downstairs and put some tea and food for your husband and baby, and then I'll come and talk to you." The thought of losing the best domestic she had ever employed was quite shocking for Lois's mistress, but a possible solution was already forming in her mind. As well as Lois she employed outside help; for her garden, and window-cleaning, and odd repair jobs. If Lois's husband was the right sort she would employ them both. Her house was far too big. They could have a bed-sitting room and use of the kitchen for meals without impinging on her privacy, and for accommodating the baby she could offer them less than the usual wage. Getting a very favourable impression of the young husband, she made them her offer — he to be a live-in gardener, window-cleaner, and odd-job man, and Lois to continue as before. She gave them the half-hour before the last train left to think it over.

To go back home to semi-starvation but to be free

creatures in their own humble place, or to enter the gate of servitude with its advantages for their child, — the dilemma left him little choice. "I'll come, Lois", he said shortly, and then she knew how great his love for them both was.

The strike went on a few months more, but the miners lost their hopeless battle and gave in to the grinding hardship of their daily lives. But Uncle Bill and Auntie Lois never came back to live in the Forest again.

CHAPTER
FOUR

The villagers struggled to gather up the strands of their threadbare existence. A few men, my father prominently among them, who had been outspoken leaders of the strike, were now banned from the pithead. The terrible struggle of this handful of families to survive for the next few years, including our own family, still brings intolerably painful memories made bearable by recalling the kindnesses of many hard-pressed friends and neighbours.

At the end of the strike all the village pig-sties were empty. There was no money to feed a pig. The flitch of bacon which normally hung on the walls for winter eating was sadly missed. Mostly it was only one flitch anyway; the other would have gone to the grocer to pay for the bran to help rear it. The year before the strike we had been a two-pig family. Someone had given Mam two weakling runts for whom the over-fecund sow had no spare teats. Mam lived up to her reputation, and turned them into fat pink squealers. They were almost ready for the butcher when our village began to plunge into the post-war economic doldrums that make today's recession look like wild prosperity. Tradesmen were loath to give any more on tick. Many families were desperate.

Then one of the cottagers had the idea of taking his pig to sell at Gloucester cattle market. It would mean no flitch of bacon on the wall for the winter, but if enough pig owners went along with his notion they could hire a lorry between them and no doubt sell their pigs for a good price. The thought of a bit of ready cash was a lot better than a straw to a drowning man, and for our parents the trip would carry an extra bonus. Our dear old great-aunt had broken her hip and had been taken to Gloucester Infirmary. Taking our pigs in would give us a leg-up out of our bankruptcy *and* the chance for Mam and Dad to pay her a visit. So the project was arranged, and pigs and owners set off early on a fine late August morning with their spirits lifted.

Dad and Mam took the baby, and my twelve-year-old sister was left in charge of me and our little brother and the household chores.

"Now you do as Bess tells you and I'll bring you home a penny box of beads," Mam promised me. For this treat I was more than willing to be co-operative. These miniscule coloured beads would occupy me for ecstatic hours threading them on pieces of cotton to make rings and bracelets. Uncharacteristically I willingly did all the jobs my sister urged me to get on with. I took the bucket of grate ashes out to the ash-mix; I fetched some water from the well, and I shook the rag-mat; whilst she polished the grate, scrubbed the stone-flagged floor and made the beds. But when she came up with one of her outlandish ideas, I turned into my usual mulish self.

"We be goin' to 'ave a party, down the garden under the plum tree!" she announced.

"Ow can we 'ave a party wi' no victuals? We've only got some taters for our dinner."

"Oh, shut up, you misery-guts. You go an' ask Gladys an' Vera an' Ivy. I'll make a little fire under the plum tree and we can boil the kettle an' make some tea. An' you tell the girls they've all got to bring summat towards the picnic."

I knew this was a shrewd guest-list. Gladys was an only child with a very soft-hearted mum. She was sure to bring some bread and jam. Ivy was known to be spoiled by her two grown-up brothers and she could be counted on for at least some bread and lard. Vera, if she deigned to come, might even contribute a bit of cake, for *her* dad had a regular job on the railway; *she* was upper-crust. Lil was known to be an artful dodger. She had to be for there were twelve of them. If there was nothing in their pantry she would pinch something from the garden, like some nice juicy carrots. All the same I did not relish my errand, but a good shove and my sister's threat to tell Mam that I would not do as I was told, sent me on my way. And I got four acceptances.

When I got back my sister had built a little fire under the plum tree and was heating a saucepan of water to make the tea. She had got two boxes from Dad's shed and covered them with a tablecoth made of newspaper which she had folded and cut with little patterns and scalloped edges. In a jam jar in the middle she had arranged some flowers, but what brought me to an awestruck standstill was the teacups on the table.

28

They were Mam's treasured set, got with years of coupons cut from packets of Nectar tea. Mam had also got the teapot to match. They were never used, only proudly displayed on the shelves of Dad's home-made dresser. I thought they were ugly myself, because they were of thick, glazed pottery, dark green on the outside and brown inside, but I knew Mam thought the world of them.

"Whatever be you doin'?" I shrieked. "Our mam'll go mad if 'er knows we be usin' *them*!"

"Shut up, you sawney. 'Er won't know, will 'er. We'll put 'em back long before they do come 'ome. Now thee go 'an fetch the teapot."

But I stood my ground against such daring.

"I shan't."

"Do as I say. We can't 'ave a party wi' our old teapot; it's black from standing on the hob."

"You only want to show off. I shan't fetch it."

"All right then, an' I'll tell the girls you piddled the bed last week."

That did it; I went indoors and reached down the precious teapot. Mam kept her bills in it. I took them out and holding it gingerly in both hands I started up the garden steps. Unfortunately the new sole that Dad had just put on my boots was bringing the old one away and just caught the top of the step. I tripped up the steps and the pot went flying and landed on the path in two pieces. My blood ran cold as the magnitude of this calamity hit me. I remembered the sheer joy in Mam's face when the parcel had arrived. Now I should get the whacking of my life, and probably no beads. I began to howl. My sister came running up the path. My stricken face made her have mercy on my clumsiness.

"It was my boot," I wailed. "Look the sole's comin' off, an' it made me fall up the steps."

"Oh my gawd, now you've done it. I dunno; I reckon you'd fall over your own shadow. Now stop bellocking; I'll mend it. You know our mam can't see very well, an' when 'er do go to pick it up 'er'll think it fell to pieces in 'er 'ands."

I knew my sister was very clever, but even she could not perform miracles. Gladys and Vera were coming in through our gate. Conscious of her duties as hostess, my sister hissed at me to stop crying and spoiling the party.

"Shan't be a minute," she told them, "you two go on down under the plum tree."

I followed her into the back kitchen. She took the lump of soap from the dish, well-moistened it, and rubbed it plentifully on the jagged broken edges. Then she carefully stuck them together. It seemed to hold as she put it back on the shelf with the bills inside it, and replaced the lid which luckily had not broken. All the same it was only a half-hearted deliverance. I knew Mam's sight was very bad, and she had to hold the newspaper right up to her nose to read it. When I tried her glasses on everything looked tiny, just like the things in a doll's house. Was it bad enough to fool her with that soap? Why could not my sister have been satisfied with the old teapot? We had to use it now anyway.

I could not share her optimism despite the good spread our guests had brought; Gladys, bread and jam; Ivy, bread and dripping; some biscuits from Vera and a lump of bread pudding from Lil. I just wanted the party over and the teacups safely back on the shelf.

The teapot was still holding together on the dresser when the party was finished and the precious cups washed and put away, and we waited for the pig dealers to come home. We decided to have a game of hopscotch by the gate, and as we got there we were amazed to see Mam there carrying the baby, and Dad just behind driving the pigs home. Mam's shopping bag looked pretty empty, and she and Dad were pictures of misery.

"Whatever d'you bring 'em back for, Dad?" my little brother demanded.

Dad was grey-faced and exhausted and his tone was bitter as he lifted my brother in his arms.

"'Twas either that, my son, or practically givin' 'em away."

It seemed that nearly everyone with pigs for sale had taken them to market that day, the supply so exceeded the demand that prices had reached a ludicrous low. My sister had run indoors and got the kettle boiling on a good fire. The potatoes she had washed and put in the oven earlier on for their homecoming supper were ready. But the disappointment was like an air of mourning round the table.

Father had sunk into one of his bitter satirical moods. "Time we 'ad another war," he said to Mam, "plenty o' work down the pit then. Wages up. Top prices for pigs. Plenty o' work in the factories making armaments an' uniforms for men to die in. Seems there's nothin' like a few years o' 'uman slaughter to get the economy going." In this vein our kindly dad became a stranger in our midst.

"Did you go to see old Auntie, Dad?" my sister said, and oh! the joy to see his face light up.

"Aye, we seen your auntie. They be puttin' her 'ip to rights. An' bless 'er, them nurses do think the world on 'er. 'Er 'a' bin singin' 'em a little song:

Salts and Senna, oh how you're workin' me;
I'd rather be a butcher's boy
Than a doctor's boy I'd be.

We all ate our jacket potatoes and drank some tea. This gave Mam the stamina to breast-feed the whimpering hungry baby. Then she put her in Dad's lap, and my nerves froze as she went to the dresser with the bill they owed the pig-haulier. When she took hold of the handle of the teapot one jagged half came away in her hand. She stared at it incredulously, her face stricken with this fresh blow.

"Ave you two bin at this dresser?" she wailed. We did not answer. She picked up the other half of the teapot and peered shortsightedly along the crack. Even she could see the tell-tale soap. Should I make a dash for the door, or take my whacking now? But Mam just sat down, her spirit cracked by the events of the day, too weary and despondent to mete out our punishment. The pity I felt for her hurt more than the hard smacks I should have got on my arms and legs.

Most of the villagers were in the same sinking debt-ridden boat, but somehow they baled out and survived. Just as in city slum communities struck by a common disaster, they pulled together and overcame together. Psychiatrists earn a fat living from the rich who turn to them to unravel their emotional hang-ups. In the close-knit intimacy of village life there was not much chance for inhibitions. Marital, parental, economic and physical problems could be aired and shared, and more relief could be found than can be got on a psychiatrist's couch.

At about this time and in such arid ground it was surprising to find that we had an entrepreneur in our midst: one that could not read or write; one who was getting on a bit in years, had fathered thirteen children, twelve of whom survived, but found time on Sundays to thump the pulpit in the village chapel.

Had he been a contemporary, Lord Olivier would have had to look to his laurels, for Amos was a consummate actor. His performances always drew full congregations. He would start off with a pious gentle expression, his voice low and trembling, his arms outstretched in compassion for his errant flock. Then gradually he would work himself up into a fury over our shortcomings until his voice thundered, his eyes became blazing orbs, and his arms pointed to the pit of hellfire that surely awaited the sinners who did not seek redemption.

Churchill's famous remark could have applied to him for he often became intoxicated by his own verbosity and did not know when to stop. Luckily we always had Mr Watson in the audience and when the sermon had gone on long enough he could wait for Amos to draw breath and then interject a couple of sonorous "Amens".

This was the signal for the organist to get quickly on his stool and play the closing hymn. Then having had

Amos make all that effort on our behalf, pleading for our previous week's sins to be forgiven, we would file out of chapel and provide him with more ammunition for the next Sunday.

Amos however, did not believe that charity began at home. He held the purse-strings in his family. Sometimes on Saturday I walked with one of his young daughters the couple of miles to town to do him some shopping. He had six sons and six daughters — as soon as they were old enough the girls went into service and the boys down the pit. His daughter always had to buy eight herrings, two for Amos and one each for the boys; his wife and his young daughters still at home were of not enough significance to get one.

He was not so mean, however, as one of my own ancestors, a regular scat of a father, who was reputed to offer his sons a penny each for going without their suppers and charge them a penny each for their breakfasts.

Anyway, old Amos always had a shilling or two in his pockets, and when one day the chance came for him to buy a second-hand circular push-bench saw with a diesel engine, at a fraction of its real value, he nabbed it. With the help of a couple of his sons he built a wooden shelter on a piece of waste ground at the bottom of the village and installed his saw bench, With pit-work so scarce he was soon making a living cutting firewood logs, and seeking orders from the farmers for stakes and wood fencing. He bought his material from the Forestry Commission, and it must have been a bargain for Amos was soon prospering.

When work improved in the mines he got contracts for props, lids, cogs and sleepers. His sons were strong, hardworking young men; the herrings must have done them good. Soon he was employing two that were already married and a couple of the older of those still at home. Business flourished, and by the time he was in his early sixties he had a proper little sawmill. He still could not read or write but he could count up money all right, and the village reckoned he had plenty to count.

Then into his garden of Eden came temptation in the nubile form of a seventeen-year-old girl with her eyes open looking for a sugar-daddy, a rival winning over his religious fervour. He lost all interest in the chapel and the pulpit.

Secrets had a short life in our village. The tongues were soon wagging and saintly old Amos became the dirty old devil. Tongues wagged even harder when Amos had a fine caravan put alongside his sawmill and everybody could have been "knocked down wi' a feather" when he moved into it with his youthful concubine.

"Disgraceful", "no fool like an old fool", "fancy shittin' on 'is own doorstep like that!" The village washed their hands of him, and turned their sympathy on to his wife and daughters who had washed their hands of him too.

After bearing him thirteen children, and putting up with his parsimony, his gentle long-suffering wife was sorry to be rid of his masculinity. But the humiliations of his downfall from grace, and the slight to her status as his wife and mother of his children, were hard for her to bear and she did not live much longer.

But men are men. The sons did not like their father's behaviour but they had worked very hard to help build up the business. Their livelihood was in his hands. Some of them now had their own dependent families. They loved their mother and made it plain to her while they put up with the sins of the father.

Shunned and ignored by the villagers he enjoyed his life in his illicit love-nest to a ripe old age. When he died, his was the one soul that the chapel-goers did not pray for. After all the warnings he had given them about hellfire, he above all should have known better than to court the devil.

Without the bonus of a young body to keep his old bones warm, and without the affluence of Amos, his cousin Jacob struggled on into his late eighties, but by then he had had enough of longevity.

"I don't mind not bein' able to zee much, nor 'ear much, nor 'avin' no tith left in me chops to chew me victuals, but now me legs an' arms be givin' up on me I be good fer nothin'!"

As the Lord seemed reluctant to call him old Jacob decided he would have to take matters into his own hands. He lived with his son and daughter-in-law. One morning after his son had gone off to his early shift at the pit and his daughter-in-law slept on, he hobbled downstairs for his cut-throat razor. Creeping back as quietly as he could he made himself comfortable in bed and proceeded to cut his throat. In his frail and trembling old hands it was more of a job than he had anticipated. When his daughter-in-law brought him a cup of tea he was bleeding badly and exhausted by the effort. The sight sent her screaming to the neighbours for help.

The doctor was fetched, and old Jacob was taken to the hospital to be stitched up and nursed. He was not a grateful patient, but he recovered reluctantly and was sent home.

In the little time that was actually left to him he often cursed his inefficiency. "I'll make sure I do the bloody job all right next time," he would say. But razors and knives were kept out of his way, and in a few weeks he had no further need of them.

CHAPTER
FIVE

Being taken advantage of by mean and wily people is part of the bitter brew of living. But there are plenty of spoons of sugar to sweeten it in the actions of the generous and the kindly-disposed. Mam had a huge sweetener when her seventh baby was a few months old and someone gave her a pushchair. It quite went to her head. Hitherto, if Dad was not available she had carried her babies Welsh-fashion, in a big shawl round her shoulder.

Of the seven, four of us had survived, and there was still a sister to come. The pushchair had solid iron wheels and its seat and back were fashioned from a piece of carpet.

Now she had some transport Mam had thought of a treat for us. "If you'll all be good young 'uns an' it's a nice day Sunday, I'll take you all down to the river Wye for a picnic."

I had seen the Wye a year previously, but its only interest to me then was that it was liquid . . . I was ill and had developed an abnormal thirst, and despite all the scoldings and advice I drank anything I could get hold of, sneaking into the back-kitchen to take from the pans of water that had been carried with much labour from the well by the main road; popping into Granny's next door when she went up her garden and drinking the slops left in the teacups. There was no stopping me. I lost weight and began to develop sores, especially on my legs. There was nothing else for it; Mam would have to take me to the doctor, and this was a decision not to be taken lightly.

In those pre-National Health Service days it was the custom for poor families to pay five shillings a quarter for the doctor's services. These payments were frequently in arrears, so Dad's herbal brews, spoonfuls of brimstone and treacle, goose-grease and Nature herself usually managed the cures. But not this time, so Mam had to scrape up a shilling off the arrears and walk me the two miles to the doctor's. Old Auntie that we lived with, and Granny, minded the other children.

By the time we had walked through the woods to the main road my raging thirst got me running to the horse-trough, with Mam struggling to pull me away. She had to struggle even harder when we got to Waterloo Pit at the top of Lydbrook where recent rain had left puddles in the road. Down I went on hands and knees and despite Mam's tearful remonstrances scooped the water into my mouth.

Lydbrook is built on each side of a valley road that leads down to the banks of the Wye. The doctor's house was almost at the bottom, and I could see the river just across the road. Some years at this point the Wye floods, showing no respect even for the doctor's big house where the lower walls were stained with the overflow. Mam marched me into the waiting room. We came out with a box of ointment and a big bottle of medicine.

If Dad was not about I liked Granny to put the ointment on my sores. She was so gentle and tried not to hurt. Maybe her salty tears, which fell in my sores as she was doing it, acted as an extra antiseptic. The medicine and the ointment soon cured the condition, for, as one of our neighbours observed who was called in to get the medicine down my reluctant gullet, "the devil do look after his own."

Now this new prospect of going down to the river was different. I could look upon the Wye without wanting to drink it dry. Early on Sunday morning my big sister poked me out of bed. Mam lined the pushchair with feather pillows from the bed and tied the baby in with an old scarf. We took turns carrying the bag with the picnic — my sister mostly. She was thirteen and would soon be going into domestic service in Bristol, where one of our Aunties had spoken for her a job as a general maid to two elderly ladies. We were a proud little convoy as we negotiated the pushchair down the steep rutted village track to the main road. Mam had prepared a cow's heart, cabbage and potatoes for old Auntie to cook for our supper instead of having it for our dinner.

Half a mile along the main road we came to the cross-roads where a turning led to Waterloo Pit and Lydbrook, but to our surprise Mam did not take it. Instead we carried on, and up a long steep hill to a turning on the right through the Forest. Soon the woodland petered out into a gentle valley with farmland either side. Down in the valley by the side of the path we found an empty cottage, its abandoned garden now a jungle of weeds.

"Come on," my sister encouraged me, and we were soon foraging among the weeds in case there was a bush left with something edible on it. We found nothing, and no hidden treasure lying about either, and a peep through the bare windows revealed a very humble dwelling stripped to its stone flagged floors and distempered walls. Disappointed but not too dismayed we soon caught up with Mam and the baby and our little brother. Then Mam spotted a field of swedes, not yet ready to harvest but big enough for some juicy bites.

"See if you can get through the hedge somewhere an' pull a couple," said Mam who had no scruples where a field of swedes and her hungry offspring were concerned.

We soon obliged. Mam rubbed off as much dirt as she could on the grass verge, took the knife she had brought to cut up our picnic loaf, and peeled us a big wedge each. We ignored the smears of earth. "You 'a' got to eat a peck o' dirt 'afore you die" was a common adage. The firm and juicy pale orange flesh was a joy to munch.

Now we had come to the bottom of the valley and began to climb up to the top. Poor Mam! Childbearing and work had left her thin little legs a mass of varicose veins. My sister took over the pushchair.

"Oh, look at that!" exclaimed Mam as we came upon a vista of beautiful flowers and lawns fronting a big house. Gardening was Mam's joy and she was passionately fond of flowers. "I wish I could 'ave a slip or two o' some 'o they flowering shrubs," she said wistfully. Mam truly had green fingers; ignoring the right season or the nature of the plant, if she could get a slip of something she fancied, she would put it in the ground with a bit of compost under it, lovingly firming it in, and away it would grow.

I remember one day we found a piece of a broken walking stick, and I asked Dad what sort of wood it was. He gave the subject his usual close attention but admitted he could not recognise it. Then he said, "Why not give it to your Mam? If she sticks it in the garden it'll be sure to spurt into summat, an' then we'll know!"

But this time Mam looked longingly at the shrubs around the big house in vain. None of us would dare to cross those tailored lawns. As we went slowly by I could see through one of the huge french windows a capped and aproned maid dusting the furniture. Fancy having to be stuck indoors on a day like this, dusting! But I knew that as soon as I left school the same fate awaited me. But did it? And I went into one of my daydreams.

I knew that the elderly midwife brought the new babies and left them under a gooseberry bush in the garden of the house where they belonged. What if the midwife had made a mistake with me? After all she *was* very old and very busy. Perhaps she should really have left me under a gooseberry bush at this fine big house. One day soon the mistake would be discovered and I would become the long-lost child of the rich parents who lived here. Every day I would wear silk dresses with flounces, and white shoes and socks, I would have a doll with curls to play with, and lovely things like faggots and peas and tinned pineapple and custard to eat for dinner and tea even on weekdays.

"Come on, slowcoach," yelled my sister, and I woke

up. Oh dear! If I really lived in this house I would not have my dad and mam, the baby, or my sister and brother. Oh, no, the midwife had not made a mistake after all! I ran to catch them up.

Only the birds in the hedgerows had kept us company through those country lanes. Now as we climbed the hill out of the valley into the attractive hamlet of English Bicknor the trees began to reappear. Soon we were on the last lap, smoothly down partly-wooded green hills, and at last came a view of the river, with a long stretch of its bank that we could have all to ourselves.

The baby had begun to whimper with the hunger we all felt, so my sister carried her about until Mam had shared out our picnic. She had brought a whole cottage loaf, a lump of cheese, some dripping in a handleless cup and a chunk of her home-made currant cake for each of us. We all took a swig and emptied one of the bottles of water she had brought.

With our energies recharged we left Mam to suckle the baby, and warned by her not to get too near the water's edge, we wandered off. Flowing water has a compelling fascination; we sat and watched the twigs and leaves on their helpless voyage. My sister had brought our empty water bottle. She picked a few leaves and some wild flowers, put them in the bottle and recorked it, then threw it into the middle of the river.

"Gawd knows where that un'll end up. It'll go right down to the Bristol Channel, then into the ocean, and maybe land in America or Africa," she said.

My sister's head was packed with brains, just like our Dad's. She was the top scholar in our little school, and just to illustrate how clever she was I will tell you something. Wireless was in its infancy, especially where we lived, and Dad was fascinated by the phenomenon of the sound waves. He bought a book about it and reckoned if he could afford the parts he could build a set. He told our groceryman this, and the grocer was inclined to believe him because everyone knew how clever and handy our dad was. So the grocer said he would give Dad some money for the parts and if he would make him one that worked all right, he would knock off some of the debt we owed for groceries.

Old Auntie slept in the little front room downstairs and Dad put a table in there with the blueprints and all the paraphernalia to make the set. This room was now barred to us children, except my sister, who was always Dad's mate when he was doing his mending jobs for us and the neighbours. I took a peep in there once and I heard them talking about coils and condensers and valves, and the soldering techniques for the wiring. One evening when Dad was on night shift at the pit, he left the partly-built set with great reluctance to get off to work.

"What be you a-doin'?" demanded Mam of my sister when she fetched a soldering iron out of the front room and put it between the bars of the fire.

"I be goin' to 'elp our Dad make that wireless."

"Don't you dare go in that room on your own or touch that set. Your Dad'll go mad!"

But my sister had a very persuasive character.

As soon as Dad came home from the pit in the early hours, and had his breakfast and washed in front of the

fire, he went into the front room. He stared unbelieving-
ly at the progress made on his wireless set. The blueprint
had been followed with all the skill he could have
achieved for himself.

"Don't blame me," wailed Mam suspecting the worst,
"'er's that headstrong. I couldn't stop 'er. You can get
'er out of bed an' correct 'er yourself."

Dad was in a dilemma. He was very proud of this
multi-gifted daughter, but angry with her for disobeying
him; *nobody* was to touch anything on that table. So she
got her meed of praise and a bigger one of disapproval
to go with it. But as he said out of her hearing, what
could you do with a wench that could turn out a chair leg
on his lathe just as well as he could? "Er should 'a' been
a boy," was his chauvinistic comment.

Further down the bank a lone fisherman was casting
his line in the river, and my sister took our little brother
down to watch him. Now I was alone I could call quietly
down into the river to see if a goddess named Persephone lived under it. Sometimes one of my aunties
would bring home from her job some unwanted books.
There was a coverless copy of Wordsworth's poems
which I struggled to read and understand; especially one
called the "May Queen". I did not understand it, but it
had a sad cadence that made me wallow in moods of
melancholy. Also there was one on Greek mythology
which had in it a woman called a Gorgon with snakes
instead of hair, and this one gave me the horrors. But I
liked best a story about a goddess named Persephone
who lived under the water. Oh, I wished my name was
Persephone; it sounded so pretty. Perhaps she lived

under the Wye now, and would come up and see me if no one else was about. But all my cajoling brought no response.

I wandered down to watch the fisherman. He had no luck either. If he had caught a salmon he would have had to throw it back. My sister said all the salmon in that part of the river belonged to Cardinal Vaughan's estate on the other bank. He was a Catholic, and had his own church built beside his mansion. "And what's more," my sister said, "he's got a bloody cheek to claim the salmon. It was God who put them in the river, not him."

By the time Mam called us back to her our bellies were beginning to rumble again, and the thought of our supper was enough to get an obedient response to the idea of going home. This time we went the shorter way, up through Lydbrook. On our way we passed a tall old drab-looking stone cottage which stood on its own, its wall hard by the road. There was a plaque on it.

"That's where a famous actress named Sarah Siddons lived when she was a girl," my sister told us. "She went to live in London after and even acted in front of the King!"

I looked at my sister. She had long brown hair, and huge long-lashed beautiful eyes. Everyone who saw her would say what a handsome little wench she was. "Perhaps you'll be an actress when you grow up," I said.

"We homeward plod our weary way" could have been written about us as we struggled up to the top of Lydbrook. Somehow my sister found the energy to give our little brother a pick-a-back.

"I wonder if that bottle's got to the Bristol Channel

yet? D'you think it'll get to Africa? I wonder what they'll think of them flowers and leaves you put in it?" I chatted on.

"Not much," said my sister. "D'you know in the jungle rivers in Africa they a' got water lilies wi' leaves big enough for a human bein' to sit on, and they do grow things like cokernuts and bananas and pineapples over there." She knew everything, my sister did; that was because she was always with our dad.

It was uphill all the way. By the time we made the last lap up the rutted village track to home Mam was in a lather of sweat. Poor Mam! She could only give us treats that cost nothing, but this one must have cost her a lot of effort. Old Auntie had got our supper cooked, a feast to end a lovely day.

That night I had a lovely dream. I thought I was dressed like the goddess in the book, in a long white diaphanous gown, and I was floating on a big lily leaf down between the banks of the Wye.

CHAPTER
SIX

One day when I ran in from play, there was our mam, and old Auntie and Granny, all looking very dejected and as though they had been crying.

"Whatever's the matter?" I demanded.

"'Tis poor old Louie," answered Granny, "they 'ave come an' took 'er to the work'ouse."

I knew what that meant. She had gone to Westbury, and that was a name often on the minds and sighs of the old folk. For, above all, they dreaded the humiliation of ending their days there.

Old Louie had children, but their own hearths were too crowded and their purses too thin to accommodate their old widowed mother. To find room and service for a geriatric was physically impossible in crowded cottages with no indoor sanitation, a privy down the garden, and taps and sinks unheard of.

"'Er won't trouble 'em for long," said old Auntie, "this'll break 'er 'eart."

I too was sorry that old Louie was going from her little cottage. Sometimes Mam would give me a spare cabbage or a bit of rice pudding to take to the old lady, and I would empty her bucket of grate ashes on to the ash-mix just outside her gate, and sometimes run an errand for her. Then I could sit on her fender and listen to her talk of the old times when she was young. It was hard to believe that old Louie had ever been young with her gummy toothless mouth, her wrinkled face, her bits of wispy grey hair, and her thin bent figure that made it a struggle for her to get even as far as her garden gate.

"I mind," she would muse, "when I went to my first job in service. I was but twelve years old, and o' course I didn't know nothin' o' the ways o' the gentry. Not that they were real gentry, just a stuckup pair wi' a drapery shop. 'Twas only three miles away, but I felt that homesick, an' I did miss goin' out to play in the woods. I felt like a prisoner, stuck indoors from mornin' till night doin' 'ousework. Once a week I 'ad time off to go 'ome, but by the time I'd walked there 'twas nearly time to start walkin' back again. I cried like a great gawbee the first time when it was time to go back. But I stuck it there for two years. Then I got a good job at the doctor's house. I left there to get married when I was twenty. Doesn't thee be in a 'urry to get married, my wench; 'tis Nature's trick.

"I thought 'twere a 'appy release to get out o' service but it turned out little better than jumping out o' the fryin' pan into the fire. 'Twas all right in the beginning 'afore the babbies started to come along an' the pit wages 'ouldn't stretch to keep us all.

"Still, when I was first married I did 'ave a few 'apence in me purse, an' one day a few of us got together an' we hired the carrier to take us into Gloucester for the day in 'is 'orse 'n cart, an' then go to Barton Fair there in the evenin'. What a day that was, my wench! As we went through Longhope the plum trees was 'anging over the road, an' we stood up in the cart an' picked the ripe plums as we went along. The carrier changed 'orses at the Red Lion in Huntley, then we rode on to the Dog Inn just this side o' Gloucester. 'Twas all of eighteen mile! 'Im left 'is 'orse 'n cart there an' we walked into Gloucester.

"Up Westgate Street to the Cross, an' I could 'a' stood there all day gawpin' at the people. The Cross is where the four main streets do meet, Northgate, Southgate, Eastgate an' Westgate. I never imagined such crowds an' such comin's and goin's. Some o' the women was dressed up like royalty! An' oh! the shops, my wench. Why, there was frocks in some o' the windows would a' took two months o' my man's wages to pay for. But there was ragged little children too, runnin' about barefoot an' tryin' to do a bit o' beggin' on the quiet.

"The carrier knowed Gloucester well, and 'im took us about. We went to the jam factory. 'Twas more like a great lean-to shed wi' no front on it, Men were stood on a platform wi' wooden spoons far bigger than garden spades stirrin' the jam in great big iron coppers big enough to drown in. An' from what I could see o' the plums that was goin' they wasn't fussy about the bad 'uns, or them as the wasps 'ad been in, nor a few sticks an' leaves in among 'em.

"Then we went to a pot-house for our dinner, an' a fine dinner it was. You could watch 'em cuttin' the meat for your plates off great sirloins o' beef. I was glad I'd 'ad me dinner 'afore we went to see the cattle market. After seein' them poor penned-up animals mooin' an' bleatin', for I be sure they knowed why they was there, I wouldn't a' fancied that beef good as it was, an' it seemed to be comin' back up to keck in my gullet. But then we went to t'other market, an' how I wished for a pocketful o' money! There was stalls wi' fish an' meat an' fruit, an' foreign fruit like bananas an' grapes; 'ome-made sweets 'n' cakes; an' cheap-jacks sellin' materials, bed-linen and clothes at a quarter the price the tallyman asks. But mind you, wi' some on 'em you'd 'ave to be fly not to get caught. One woman wi' us bought a pair o' dirt-cheap pillowcases, an' 'er found when 'er washed 'em they was full o'dressin', an' nothin' but a bit o' cheesecloth.

"The rest o' the party then went down to 'ave a gawp at the cathedral. 'Tis a grand place but I thought 'twould be more for your front-pew church people, not for primitive Methody chapel-goers the likes o' we. Meself I don't even fancy goin' to church, it's too proud for me. The somebodies wi' money that do claim the front pews don't want to mix wi' the rest o' the congregation. I do wonder on times 'ow things be managed in 'eaven! I don't think it would suit the grand sort if we was all lumped together.

"But I 'ad me Cousin Tilly's address in me pocket, and the carrier showed me 'ow to get there. 'Twas down an alley place of Westgate Street not far from the Cathedral, an' to tell the truth I was glad I didn't take any of the other women wi' me. 'Twas a shock, I can tell you. I thought 'er was set up in life when 'er left service to marry a Gloucester man an' live in a big city. The places 'ad all been condemned down that alley, but Tilly still lived in one. I knowed 'er 'ad a big family of 'er own an' a couple more 'er sister 'ad 'ad the wrong side o' the blanket, but the place seemed to be swarmin' wi' young 'uns. They didn't look as though they saw much of soap an' flannel, an' I reckon the only wash they got was when it rained, but I could see they never went short o' victuals.

"Two boys were choppin' up old boxes into bundles o' sticks; one come along wi' a big box on wheels filled wi' 'orse droppin's, an' a little wench was tyin' up bundles o' old newspapers.

"You could 'a knocked Tilly down wi' a feather when 'er saw me at the door' an' you could a' knocked me down wi' a feather when 'er asked me inside. 'Twas a tidy-sized room but very low-ceilinged wi' a little fire-place an' 'er'd papered the walls wi' bits of *Old Moore's Almanack* an' pages from magazines an' coloured papers of all sorts, like the inside of a didikoi's caravan. 'Er didn't pay rent 'cos the place was condemned. 'Er 'ad chucked 'er old man out, an' I won't repeat what 'er called 'n. There was no room for 'er to sleep upstairs; 'er managed on an old armchair by the fire. 'Er took me up the stairs. There was a little landing wi' two slop buckets on it an' a bedroom each side, one for the boys 'an one for the girls. Well, er called 'em bedrooms but they was like two long tunnels wi' iron bedsteads jam-med together all the way down. If the ones the furthest end wanted to get out o' bed to use the slop bucket, they 'ad to climb over all t'others.

"'Er biled the kettle on the fire an' made me a cup o' tea though I didn't fancy it, an' there was plenty o' victuals in 'er cupboard on the wall. They was makin' a good livin', like rats scavengin' on a rubbish tip; the boys selling the 'orse manure to big 'ouses for their gardens, an' their bundles of sticks, and papers, rags and bones to the rag-and-bone shop. An' mind you, they didn't leave anything lyin' about anywhere wi'out an eye to it.

"I could see the little 'uns loved 'er for they was climbin' up on 'er lap an' puttin' their arms round 'er neck' an', took aback as I was I still thought those young 'uns was better off than if they'd been put in a work'ouse. They'd 'a' been kep' clean but they wouldn't 'ave 'ad the love, nor such good victuals in 'em. The authorities left Tilly alone — they'd been there once or twice, but Tilly's tongue, an' 'er could cuss a bit, drove 'em off.

"But I could see 'er 'ad took to the gin a bit. I saw 'er take a swig or two out the bottle while I was there, but who could blame 'er? I give the young 'uns the bag o' humbugs I'd bought in the market, an' then I went down to meet t'others outside the Cathedral, an' we all went to Barton Fair.

"There was enough things there to make your eyes pop out o' your 'ead! As well as swings and roundabouts and cokernut shies an' such like, there was the world's fattest man and woman, a five-legged pig, lions in a cage, fortune-tellers, an' dancin' bears; an' then I don't reckon we saw the 'alf of it! That's a place you do want to go when you do grow up, my wench, Gloucester! It 'a' got everything."

Poor old Louie! Now she would have to lie in bed in

the workhouse and wear one of their stiff calico night-gowns, and look through the window at the orchards and lands of the great house of Westbury Court, and wait to die.

I started to sniffle myself, but Granny had the cure. "Thee go into my pantry, my wench," said Granny, "there's a piece o' bread puddin' on a plate in there. Thee can 'ave it." And I was off.

There were two elderly brothers, bachelors, living together in the nearby forest. They had ensured that a fate like poor old Louie's should not befall them. They lived in one of the isolated and primitive cottages dotted about in the thick of the woods. They had worked in the pit until they were seventy, saving a nest-egg from their frugal wages, and augmenting it with what they could glean from the Forest and what they could grow in their well-cultivated garden. They mixed very little with other folk, and few sought them out, for they were gruff of nature and not socially inclined. But Old Father Time kept an eye on them, and when they were in their eighties one of the brothers fell ill with severe bronchial trouble aggravated by his years of work underground. So his brother trudged off to fetch the doctor.

Now the doctor himself was well past normal retiring age and in his late seventies. So he was not too happy at the prospect of leaving his pony and trap at the village inn and struggling half a mile through the woods to their cottage. However, they had always been prompt payers of his quarterly fee.

By the time he got to their cottage the old doctor was

wheezing pretty bad himself. The patient was in a bad way; it would be touch and go if he recovered and without the doctor actually saying so, the ill man sensed this. He was still game of spirit and managed to threaten the doctor that he would see *him* out yet.

He made a partial recovery, but about a year later his strength waned till he had to take to his bed again; as Shakespeare says, sans teeth, sans hair, sans appetite, sans almost everything. The doctor was fetched in by the brother yet again, but this time medicine and advice could do no good. In confidence the doctor told the able brother that on medical evidence his brother should no longer be in the land of the living, but once again the sick man managed to threaten the doctor that he would see him out yet!

Caring for the helpless invalid, brother or no, was a great burden to the other. If it was Ben's time to go then Ben ought to go, he thought.

Sentiment had found sparse nourishment in their hard lives. Nature had instilled her message; when it has had its season everything must die. They were not chapel-goers, and once when an enthusiastic newly-appointed vicar had called to persuade them into his flock with the promise of everlasting life, old Ben had taken him into the garden. He had shown the vicar a dead rose ready to drop from its stem.

"Thic rose be dyud, Vicar, an' finished. Next year ther'll be some new 'uns an' that's 'ow it be wi' 'uman beins. When we be put under the ground that's the finish o' we, but there's allus plenty o' young 'uns to take our places."

Now Ben was a long time dropping from his stem. He was no help and no company, and it was all his brother could do to manage for himself, leave alone caring for another. A flavour of irritation crept into the relationship from Ben's inconsiderate hanging on to an existence that no longer had any meaning. There was no question of him letting them cart Ben off to the workhouse; that would be unthinkable. No, Ben should oblige him and the doctor and realise the time had come to give up the ghost; and one morning this was what he thought Ben had done.

There was no response from the still and emaciated figure in the bed; not even for a sip from the spoonful of spring water which was all he had shown the inclination to swallow for the previous two days. Poor old Ben! 'Im was gone at last! But now the doctor must be fetched yet again for the death certificate.

The two relieved old men plodded their way back to the cottage. The old doctor looked down at the corpse. His own reflexes were not too good, but satisfied that the end had come he stood in respect with the brother by the bed.

"Ah, yes. Your brother's gone to his maker at last; God rest his soul."

But then the head on the bed made a hardly perceptible movement, and a weak voice croaked, "I bain't dyud, Doctor, I still be'ere."

Stung to retort by this obstinacy, his brother admonished him, "Now thee shut up, Ben; doosn't argue wi' the doctor. 'Im do know best."

Next evening as the brother was fetching a bucket of

water from the spring, a passing Forest worker gave him the news. They had found the old doctor dead in bed that very morning.

When his young replacement called a couple of days later there was no arguing from Ben.

"I knowed 'im 'ouldn't be any trouble to you, Doctor, for when I 'eard the old doctor was gone I shouted the news in each of Ben's ear'oles, an' that must 'a satisfied 'im. 'Im was determined to last out the longest o' them two.

CHAPTER
SEVEN

As soon as we are born we become passengers on the train of time. Time, that indescribable element, all-powerful, yet cannot be recognised by any of our five senses. Unstoppable, it carries us on to our destiny. We measure it by the sun and the stars and the seasons. Each turn of this Earth we call a year, and when my fourteenth year arrived the custom of necessity in our village life sent me out into the great wide world to earn my living as a domestic servant, as I have described in *Child in the Forest*. The heartache and worry it must have caused our parents; having to let us go with only their love and our natural instinct to survive to protect us from the temptations most of us were still ignorant of. It is a compliment to the esteem that such girls felt for their parents, that so very few fell by the wayside.

Looking back on my own past I remembered a time when I too might have gone the wrong way. I too teetered on the edge of the slippery slope. As green in experience as the flora in my beloved Forest of Dean, I had taken a job in a bed-and-breakfast boarding house near Paddington station. My mistress was the daughter of a very religious man who had a business in the suburbs. He rented this house at a high figure from the

Ecclesiastical Commissioners who owned the whole terrace, a terrace of such ill repute that they should have sent a squad of missionaries there to save the lost souls.

I soon learned not to use my master key to clean the bedrooms of the male boarders unless I was sure they were out. There were occasional exceptions. Sometimes rooms were let to young men, mostly in the acting profession, soft-voiced, giggly people who behaved to me as perfect gentlemen, and often had a member of their own sex in bed with them in the morning. One of my principal aggravations was an Egyptian doctor, a dermatologist, over in England to attend a conference on skin diseases. I soon learned to leave his breakfast tray just outside his door to prevent him grabbing me from the bed if I put it down on the bedside table.

One evening he rang his bell quite late for a pot of tea and toast, the only extra that we served. I thought that he was looking for an extra extra so I stayed on the landing for him to take the tray. He had a glass of red wine in his hand and tried very hard to cajole me inside to drink. I stood my ground, but to shut him up when the next door was opened by a curious occupant I drank the wine and went back to the kitchen.

To the kitchen? To the usual old dark miserable basement kitchen? Not a bit of it. It had suddenly become a lovely place; all the world was lovely; everything was so funny and beautiful and relaxed. My legs began to give way. I sat on the hard kitchen chair, and fell off convulsed with laughter. I lay on the floor in a helpless state of happy euphoria. But the noise of the chair falling over and my giggling brought the mistress into the kitchen.

The big room in the front part of the basement was her bed-sitting room and she had already gone to bed.

"Have you gone mad? Whatever's the matter with you? Pull yourself together, acting like a fool this time of night. Get yourself into bed, or I'll give you notice." This threat only increased my paroxysms of laughter. I did not care. I did not care about anything. I was just utterly relaxed in mind and body.

"Get yourself to bed; you must be hysterical," she snapped, and took herself off. I managed to stagger into my bedroom, but only to have a gloriously funny fight with my clothes, my pyjamas, and the bed, all of which had become contortionists. I awoke about three in the morning with the most dreadful thumping headache and nausea.

The next day he had the sauce to offer me another glass, but with true Eliza Dolittle spirit I told him angrily, "Not bloody likely," and to stop pestering me. I shuddered to think what could have happened if I had drunk his concoction inside his room that evening.

Perhaps it was the hot climate they came from, but the Eastern gentlemen made the most determined onslaughts on my virginity. I became quite adept at dodging one particular fat middle-aged fellow whom I had nick-named "bum-washer". Every time I saw him emerging from the lavatory he was carrying a bowl of warm water.

He never answered my knocks on his door so that I was frequently pinned up against the wall or even pushed on to his bed whence I had to fight him off. This occupational hazard was a regular occurrence and I was getting used to it.

60

Oddly enough it was this gentleman who inadvertently gave me a push in the wrong direction. On the whole my mistress was an easy-going employer. She went out a lot, taking her little rag-bag of a chihuahua dog for a walk, going into Lyons teashops for nosh-ups, and taking out her aggravation on any totter or roundsman with a horse and cart. In her eyes all horses were ill-treated creatures. If the equine population was a bit thin on the ground she took her bile out on me, with sudden inspections of the tenants' rooms.

One day I had already cleaned out the six shared bathrooms, but old "bum-washer" had used one afterwards and had left a tide mark of greasy oil and black hairs adhering to the side of the bath. Moreover, there was fluff under his bed, and all the wardrobes had thick dust on the top.

She was in no mood to listen to my complaints about dodging the attentions of her boarders, and in truth I was not a born domestic. If the dust kept out of sight I was willing to forget it. At the time scientists had not brought close-up pictures on television screens of the billions of microbic horrors that abound in neglected corners. Anyway I had far too much to do. Aggrieved, and near to tears that were a mixture of anger and self-pity, I flounced about in a sweat till I had pacified her and gladly saw the back of her through the front door.

I still had the boiler to rake free of cinders, I still had the kitchen floor and basement passage to scrub, pepper and salt pots to fill and eighteen breakfast trays to lay out. I was sick up to my eyes of being a skivvy. What a lot in life!

As all this was running through my mind there came a welcome distraction. Miss Staples from the ground-floor back room came down to the kitchen and ordered a pot of tea and toast, and I was flattered when she said she would have it in the kitchen to keep me company.

Miss Staples had been there a few weeks. I had been very impressed when she had rung the front doorbell and enquired for the room to let. She was dark, good-looking, slim and elegant, and wore a fur coat. As I did not know mink from musquash, I did not know that it was coney, and the bare patches under the arms did not show. She had a strong Welsh accent and a rather effusive friendly manner. She was a night-club hostess; we had had a couple of those before, but Miss Staples was different. I was convinced of her respectability because I often overheard her singing to herself the hymns we sang in the village chapel back home.

I deeply envied her her way of life. She could lie abed until midday, then dress up and go out for the afternoon, often coming in with one of her male Welsh relations. An elderly uncle, nephew, cousin or maybe just an ex-neighbour. There must have been a dearth of men in Tonypandy at the time, and most of them must have been related to Miss Staples and migrated to London. They never stopped long, and she often sang after they had gone.

About half-past ten or eleven o'clock at night, made up to the nines and wearing evening dress, she would go off to her job in Piccadilly. What a contrast to my own existence of drudgery on ten shillings a week, and she could wear a fur coat and smart clothes, eat her lunch in a fish-and-chip shop, and go to the pictures in the afternoon if she felt like it.

I looked at Miss Staples as she sat costly drinking her tea; I thought of the miseries of my job, particularly of that very day. Why should not I be a night-club hostess? True I was no raving beauty but I had been told more than once I looked like film star Sylvia Sidney! But, but, and a little tug of reservation pulled at the back of my mind. Suddenly and tactlessly I blurted it out.

"D'you have to be a *bad* girl to be a night-club hostess, Miss Staples?"

She took no umbrage. "No indeed, you don't *have* to be a bad girl. You can make a living on the drinks if you chat the customers up well enough. You see we get the men to buy us glasses of 'pink champagne'. It's only Tizer pop really. The manageress charges them half a crown a glass, it's only worth a ha'penny, and the hostess gets sixpence a glass commission. It's ninepence on their beer, and two bob if you persuade 'em to buy whisky. Of course they're overcharged a mile for it!"

"How on earth," I asked, "can they get customers if they cheat them like that?"

"Oh well, they're usually half-cut before they come in. The manageress employs a couple of touts to go round the West End pubs. They can pick the customers out. They ask them if they want to see a naked woman. It's only a big picture of a naked woman hung up in the club, but once the hostesses start chatting them up they don't care."

Oh well, I thought, they were probably rich men daft enough to throw their money about. Still on the boil from my telling off I told her how I wished I could be a night-club hostess, and did she think she might get me a job in her club? She seemed a bit dubious but said she would try for me. I could hardly believe my luck when she told me the next day that the manageress was willing to take me on trial.

Instead of the usual half-day off per week and every other Sunday afternoon I was given free time from seven pm every other evening. I had my own front-door key, and as long as I was up early for work my mistress did not care what time I came in. So I could go to the night-club. But there was still a snag; I had no evening clothes and no money to buy them.

"Call me Lily," Miss Staples had said. So I did, and Lily sorted through her wardrobe to fit me up. I was considerably more nubile than she, and a couple of inches taller, but I got into a skin-tight blue satin evening dress and with even more difficulty coaxed my sturdy feet into shoes that were little more than high heels and silver straps. Sophistication was applied with rouge, eye-shadow, mascara, powder and lipstick. Then a short fur cape of dubious origin, and I thought I was a sensation. But London did not bat an eyelid as I teetered my way with Lily down to the bus stop in Edgware Road.

However the bus conductor squeezed my hand and pinched my bum; a sign, I thought, that I was on my way to becoming a *femme fatale*! Actually we were on our way to Ham Yard near Piccadilly Circus. I squeezed Lily's arm as we got off the bus. "Oh, you are good to be such a friend to me." My imagination was working overtime. I had only seen night-clubs on the screen, lush places where Fred Astaire and Ginger Rogers danced or Betty Grable sang and pirouetted. I did not expect anything as grand as *that*, but Ham Yard with its smelly dustbins, and its empty boxes and cartons strewn about its ancient cobbles, and its general insalubrious air, was a dreadful disappointment. Yet this was only a hint of the shocks to come.

My disillusionment was self-inflicted. All my life, even as a child, I had dodged reality, daydreaming of a rosy future for myself. I had also learned to adjust, but now it was impossible to bridge the gap between my anticipations and the tiny cloakroom Lily took me to just inside the club door, to take our coats off and dab on a bit more make-up. It was squalid and dingy, with a fly-blown mirror over a little table that was covered in spilt face powder, and a lavatory and washbasin sadly crying out for some Vim and hot suds. The walls and ceiling were well coated with London grime. I was speechless but Lily seemed unaware of it all.

Then we went into the club. This was a large oblong room, probably converted from a mews stable. At one end a fire burned, and in front of it were grouped some tables and chairs. On a wooden dais at the other end of the room three shabby down-at-heel musicians waited with their instruments. On the wall hung a large picture of a naked woman. It may have been pornographic, but pornography was a closed book to me then. The manageress came up to us, and I did not take to her any more than to the surroundings. She was a hard-faced peroxide blonde, and I felt intimidated even before she opened her mouth. I was to sit up in the corner by the so-called band and wait my turn for a customer. I would be last in the queue, so I could watch the other hostesses and learn a few tips. Three or four of these had arrived and were already sitting round the fire. I had never seen anything like them in the streets in daylight. I thought they looked like painted corpses. Something was missing from their heavily mascaraed eyes. Their spirits had died and left them. Lily seemed a humane and superior being altogether. Bewildered and apprehensive I went and sat in the far corner. I could hear the bandsmen talking crudely about the feminine potentialities of the young Judy Garland.

Presently a tout came in with four customers; no dinner-jacketed, starch-fronted, bow-tied, habitués of the films. No, these looked just like the miners from our village in their best navy serge suits and white mufflers, when they had an outing to London to see a football match! Like wound-up puppets the hostesses came to life. Their false vivacity, smiles and laughter made me cringe. The men were the worse for drink. I had been in this place only half an hour, but I was already completely certain that I was never going to do this job. Never. But how to get out? The terrifying manageress was between me and the door. I was too nervous to walk past her. Drinks were already being ordered by persuasion, but it was not yet Lily's turn for a customer. I caught her eye and beckoned her over.

"Oh Lily, I want to get out of here. I don't want to be a hostess. I'd never be any good at it!"

Lily did not seem surprised. "That's okay," she said, "come with me. I'll tell the manageress you want to go to the toilet. Come on, she's busy anyway."

We slipped quietly out. As I put on Lily's borrowed coat, she put hers on too, and we emerged into the comparative fresh air of Ham Yard. My evening of glamour was over, my night-club career was ended before it had begun, but the evening's surprises were not finished.

"I'm coming with you, Win," said Lily. "Oh, how ashamed I feel for letting you come at all! Friend you called me! Oh, Win, I'm a bad girl. Help me, Win. Help me to go straight!"

How lovely the night air of London felt to me! I would have loved to jump in the Serpentine. I felt soiled by what I had seen.

On our way home Lily poured out her life story. She and a brother and a sister had been orphaned quite young by the death of both parents from tuberculosis. Relatives had taken the children in; Lily went to a childless middle-aged uncle and aunt. The uncle was a paedophile, and was soon practising his aberration on Lily and threatening her with terrible things if she did not comply. The aunt, a staunch chapel-goer, suspected nothing. The uncle had a slight deafness which rapidly grew worse. One day when Lily was twelve years old, she was being used as the terrified victim of her uncle's obsession when her aunt returned home unexpectedly. He did not hear her, and she caught them in the sordid spectacle. There was a terrible scene. The uncle said that Lily had led him on, and now she became the victim of her aunt's unforgiving wrath. The upshot of it was that Lily was put in the workhouse, and at fourteen sent out into domestic service.

"It was a dreadful job, Win, in a rectory where there

were five children. Talk about Christians! They had me on a grindstone. I stuck it for two years, then I came to London and got a job as chambermaid in a West End hotel.

"I was a real pretty girl, Win, but I kept myself straight until a very rich man came there with his valet. This valet made a bee-line for me. He was a smashing-looking chap about twenty-eight. I started to go out with him. He bought me an engagement ring — I found out afterwards it was from Woolworth's. He said he'd leave his job and we'd get married.

"Well, I got pregnant. Next thing I knew he'd gone off to America with his boss. I was destitute. I didn't know where to turn, and I thank God for the Salvation Army. They took me into one of their homes, and I had a baby girl. Oh, Win, I often wonder where she is and long to see her. After she was born I didn't care about anything; I wouldn't have cared if I'd died. When she was about six weeks old they got her adopted.

"But there must have been bad in me, Win, for I let another girl that they had taken in persuade me to go and live with her, and to be like her and get my living on the streets. I hated the thought of going back into service. I'm not very strong, Win, I've got this chesty cough and some jobs are so hard. But I *do* want to go straight. My sister's name is Winnie too; she's such a respectable girl, Win, married now with two children. They're very poor. Sometimes I send them a pound or two, but my sister would rather starve if she knew how I'd earned it."

That night it took me a long time to get to sleep.

Lily was true to her word. Lily tried. She got herself a

room in a slummy back street, and a job as a front-shop counter assistant in a Lyons Tea Shop. I followed her quickly. I gave my notice in, found a room in the same back street and a job as a Lyons nippy. Eventually Lily married a widower, fifteen years older then herself, but she coughed herself respectably into her grave some years before him.

There was another boarder there, a Miss Socrates, who was certainly not looking for salvation. She put me in mind of a porker pig caricatured into a human being. Two blue eyes were set in her fat face above a snub snout of a nose. There was an upward slant to her nostrils from her habit of wiping her nose with the back of her hand in an upward motion. Her mouth was big, full-lipped, and lascivious. She was short with fat ankles and feet, and the high-heeled shoes she always wore made them look like pig's trotters. A trough would have been a suitable receptacle for her meals. Down the front of her clothes there was always the stained residue of her slurpings.

She spoke with a thick foreign accent and described herself as a Greek interpreter and teacher. I swallowed that, and the embellishment that she was a descendant of Socrates the great philosopher, although I thought it was enough to make him turn in his grave to see such a descendant. Her "pupils" came to her room, and they were always men. They say the Greeks have a word for "it", and "it" was really Miss Socrates' stock in trade, and no branch was too crude for her to practise.

One day I saw her go out, and after a short time I went

up to clean her room. I used my master key to open the door, but she had returned. There she stood, stark-naked, behaving in front of two men in a manner that retarded my own thoughts of a sex life for some time. So that is what she was teaching! The façade was down. She still used her foreign accent, but the nearest she had been to Greece was to go through a form of marriage with a Greek washer-up to save him being deported. "Miss Socrates" was in fact Mary White from somewhere up North.

One day I was cleaning the staircase when she burst through the front door in a terrible temper and swearing obscenely about men in general and one in particular. This one had picked her up in Hyde Park and promised her seven and sixpence to sit in his car in the park. What a sit-in-the-car meant I can only imagine even now. After she had obliged he laughingly refused her the money.

"Me, I go mad. I showed ze bastard. I take off my shoe and I smash 'ees car window to pieces. Then a policeman comes, but 'ee's not get the better of Thula Socrates. No." (Much as I may like to I cannot pepper my writing with her expletives.) She stormed upstairs and slammed the door.

Presently the doorbell rang. I answered it to a young policeman enquiring for someone of her description who had just come in.

"She's going to cop it now," I thought as he went up to her room. But it was he who copped "it". She came down to the kitchen soon afterwards, her good humour quite restored. "I deed all right out o' zat deal after all. Zat policeman give me ten shillings!"

I often wonder what she taught him for that.

CHAPTER
EIGHT

If time is one of the masters of our fates, Nature is another of its dictators, and at twenty-four years old I succumbed to her demand and stepped on to the path of matrimony. It was a path strewn with emotional mine-fields, jealousy, ecstasy, heartache and responsibilities, as two individuals held each other's hands to escape the pitfalls on the way.

It was nineteen thirty-eight, and I had known Syd for a couple of years. We had shared great childhood poverty in common, mine in the Forest, his in the slums of Paddington. We also shared a hatred of war and of the ethics of capitalism. I had benefited from the influence of a remarkably intelligent and good father, but Syd's dad had died when he was only two, leaving his mother a young widow with three children; a girl, a year older who died and a sister three years older who grew into a beautiful and kindly girl with whom I was much impressed.

These three survivors had lived in one room in a street of slum property owned by Lord Portman. Syd's mother got married again, to a soldier who had served his time in India; a bad tempered drunkard more out of work than in. They had then moved to a run-down area of

Kensington where they rented two rooms and a kitchen. It was a place that Syd and his sister kept away from as much as possible. Syd's sister worked as a shop assistant, and was engaged to a fine handsome ambitious fellow working his way up in a furniture shop. Syd worked as a junior clerk.

I had made a doubtful step up the social ladder. I had left my job as a living-in domestic servant and had become a room-renting waitress, the room in question being in the same shabby road that Syd lived in.

In June of 1938 we decided to get married at Christmas. Or rather, I decided. I was now twenty-four, and Syd only twenty-one, but we were two lonely creatures with few home comforts who liked each others' company. Twice Syd had been down to the Forest to meet my family, and no-one objected to the idea of our marrying. The real stumbling-block was that we were a pair of feckless idiots with no means to start married life. I was working very long hours in an Italian café in Holborn and I only managed to live on the wages by very careful scrimping. Syd's mother was always borrowing from his little bit of pocket money, so we needed all the optimism of youth to look forward to our Christmas wedding. If we went to the pictures I paid for my own sixpenny seat. If we treated ourselves to a country walk, possibly as far as Stanmore, I paid my own fare.

Now even these and other little treats had to come to an end. This did not worry us much; just living in London was a constant source of interest. As we walked through the crowded streets I was perpetually fascinated how Nature could provide such an infinite variety of faces with only the basic ingredients of two eyes, a mouth, and a nose. Syd was a bottomless source of information about historical places and people. But we had to hurry wistfully past the mouth-watering fish-and-chip shops, and the richly displayed chocolates in the confectioners' windows.

I am sure that two of the greatest pleasures for a young woman are getting things for her bottom drawer, and later on, for a coming baby's layette. I hoarded every copper I could save to spend in Woolworth's. My first purchase — for sixpence — was a wooden bread board. Another sixpence bought a saucepan, and threepence the lid. Gradually I added baking-tins, again at sixpence. In the cut-price drapers shops tea-cloths were fourpence-ha'penny, and when Syd could contribute, double sheets at five shillings the pair.

Suddenly our declining fortunes got a huge boost. My landlady's husband had gone out with the International Brigade to fight fascism in Spain's civil war. That war was just over, and as he had made no contact since his departure, she now presumed herself a widow. She had found herself a new partner and was about to move in with him. Soon she would not have my room to let, but I could buy the two chairs, the chest of drawers, the small table, and the odd bits of china and cutlery for a total of twenty-five shillings. And, if I wanted it, the piano from her own room for another five shillings.

It was a month before Christmas; every other day I had to work till midnight, so Syd set about looking for a place for us to rent. Meanwhile his mum and stepdad and his sister Flo with her fiancé Pat bought us a brand-new divan bed. Syd found two rooms off Maida Vale to let at fourteen and six per week. The landlady was a widow, and her name was Mrs Truelove which seemed a good omen. The one room was quite large and became our bed-sitting room, and the kitchen was big enough. The water-supply was a tap over a tiny sink on the stairs, and we shared the ground-floor toilet with the landlady. There was no bathroom. We could not afford the rent until we actually moved in, but for a ten-shilling deposit the place was ours.

Some of the regular customers at the cafe heard that I was getting married and began to leave tips for me, anything from twopence to sixpence. This welcome bonus was spent on curtain material; green cotton at fourpence-ha'penny a yard for the kitchen which over-looked the street, and beige flowered cretonne at sixpence a yard for the bedsitter. When I wrote home to Mam, I really enthused about making these curtains; no little hen feathering her nest could have been more excited and happy. But Syd was not quite sharing my enthusiasm for he had blotted his copybook.

We had planned a very quiet registry-office wedding, which entailed three weeks notice. Nearly at the end of the relevant Friday afternoon an office colleague of Syd's looked at his watch and said "Foley, I thought you were getting wed at Christmas!"

"That's right, I am."

"You're not, you know, registry office has just closed."

This sent Syd into a panic; how could he have

forgotten? With all the arrangements going forward as they were? My brother was borrowing a car which he was going to overhaul and repair to bring my mam and youngest sister to stay with us over the wedding. Mam was bringing a goose and a wedding-cake she had baked, and presents from the family and neighbours.

Syd was desperate. Knowing how upset I would be, never mind anything else, he followed his colleague's advice and went to see the vicar of the nearby church. I was an agnostic and Syd was a lapsed Catholic, but this Christian gentleman received us with goodwill and arranged for us to be married in church on the morning of Christmas Day. When Syd confessed his remissness to me, and told me all about it, I readily pushed my principles aside for a few days.

A couple of days before the wedding Syd's stepfather hired a coster's barrow for a shilling, and he and Syd moved the things from my rented room, and then went back for the five-shilling piano. Taking off it everything they could, somehow they got it up to our bed-sit where its bulk filled up an empty corner. There was not a single true note in it, and neither of us could play it anyway, but it did look quite grand! Meanwhile Syd received some wedding-present money from his friends at work, and we bought a square of second-hand carpet with it, and a very nice clock. I had moved in with the piano, and now I was eagerly looking forward to seeing Mam and my brother and young sister.

To drive the hundred and twenty miles from the Forest of Dean to London in nineteen thirty-eight was quite a feat. To drive it in an aged and decrepit Morris Eight with a door that had to be held shut by a suffering passenger's hand, and overloaded, and in driving sleet and snow with temperamental windscreen wipers, was a miracle. My brother was a complete stranger to London and not surprisingly he lost his bearings at Shepherd's Bush. Mother thought she was being helpful when she told him to look out for the windows with green curtains. Eventually they arrived, blue-faced and frozen with the cold. I had bought a shilling bag of coal, and soon they were thawing out round a nice fire while I fed them with the best food I could muster on our limited funds, washed down with plenty of hot sweet tea. From family and friends Mam had brought presents; table-cloths, pillow-cases, towels, a rug, and some wooden egg-cups on a stand made by my Dad which I still have.

All too soon it was time for my brother and his friend to face the horrendous hundred-and-twenty miles drive back through sleet and snow, and on icy roads. Syd called in quite late that evening. I had never seen him under the influence of alcohol, but he had been waylaid by friends for a celebratory drink. It must have been more than one, and it had turned him into a soppy good-humoured idiot. When I felt that he was capable we gave him the goose and the cake to take to his mother. The next time we would meet would be at the church, at half-past eleven on Christmas morning.

On Christmas Day there were no buses running. Luckily only a flake or two of snow fell here and there, so the mile walk to the church for the three of us was not too bad. Surprisingly another wedding had already taken place and, as everybody had left, the church looked very empty. Syd was already waiting with his best man, a lifelong friend. Syd's mum, sister, and stepdad were there but Pat had broken his leg trying to ski on Hampstead Heath, so could not come. So the tiny wedding-party was soon assembled. The vicar was waiting; there was no wedding march; I walked down the aisle in the quiet cold towards the young man who so soon would be my husband. I noticed at once that he was wearing a new suit. A new suit! It must have been a last-minute purchase, off the peg. Now Syd was, and still is, a handsome fellow; six feet tall and slightly too thin from undernourishment as a child. His new suit was too short in the sleeves, and the trousers hung well clear of his shoes. It made him look slightly ludicrous, and his thin exposed bony wrists brought a sort of maternal lump to my throat. From now on I intended to feed him properly.

The ceremony was soon over; there were no photographers; there was no confetti; just an undignified hurried dash up the road and out of the cold into Syd's mother's. The deed was done; we had cooked our goose, and how ready we were for that goose in the oven. Generous Pat had given the funds for a good supply of drinks to wash it down, and soon we were gathered round the festive table to make the most of it.

They had a gramophone and Flo had borrowed a pile of extra records to cheer up the humble occasion. Throughout the dinner Syd's stepfather got steadily drunk, and no one dared admonish him for continually refilling his glass in case he threw a fit of temper. Soon he needed to visit the toilet on the landing two flights of stairs below. Lurching helplessly from the door he stumbled across the landing, tried to hold his balance by grasping the banisters, missed and tumbled down the stairs to the next landing ending up on the pile of records and breaking almost all of them.

His drunken expletives made me look anxiously at my Mam. Whatever would she think of it all? Luckily Flo had given her a couple of glasses of sherry, and her cheeks were very rosy. She wasn't quite herself either! Flo and her mum and Syd hurried down to inspect the record-breaker. He was still breathing and apparently asleep and unharmed, so they let sleeping dogs lie and returned to the party. We chatted, played the few unbroken records, and had a cosy couple of hours, and tea and some of Mam's home-made wedding cake. As the record-breaking sleeping beauty on the landing appeared to be waking up, we thought it a tactful time for our mile walk home. Home! My new home! I was a married woman; for better or for worse! Because Mam and Marian had the bed Syd and I spent our wedding night on the kitchen floor. Mam had chatted up Mrs Truelove and borrowed some blankets for us. On Boxing Day I had to go to work, so Syd took the opportunity to show Mam and my sister a bit of London. Nothing would induce Mam to ride the moving stairs down to the underground. So they walked down and stood on the platform, well away from the edge, and awaited their train, while others shunted in, filled up and left. Totally confused by all the unfamiliar noise and bustle, Mam finally had to ask Syd if "we be there yet?" But they had not moved off the platform! My thirteen-year-old sister lapped up the bustle and novelty of it all, but poor Mam, I think she was relieved the next day to board a coach in a Paddington mews to take them back to peace and sanity.

Now Syd and I could begin our married life proper. Poor Syd! Prim and proper and prudish would be a better description. True I had reluctantly given him my virginity, but as a partner for his bed he had drawn a very short straw. Mothers like mine, struggling to bring up children they could not afford to keep, and being forced to send their fourteen-year-old daughters out into the world, used every ploy to try to keep their girls away from the temptations of the flesh. Sex was almost a taboo subject, associated with guilt, men, and the devil. They meant well, but they created a psychological chastity-belt that would take years to shed. And Syd was not exactly a Lothario himself, inexperienced and hounded by the dogmas of his Catholic upbringing, still afraid of a Hell that was pushed into his mind when he was three years old. But we survived our shortcomings and we discovered our compensations.

I filled Syd's stomach with good food, and he filled my brain with rich pickings from his. Despite his disadvantaged childhood, Syd had managed to pass the exams to an excellent Catholic grammar school. He made good progress there, but when he was seventeen his stepfather resented him staying on at school so much that he left. He was an omnivorous reader, but above all a thinker. Coupled with genuine concern for his fellow-men it was inevitable that his politics should lean heavily to the left and he hated the stupidity of war. On these two matters we were in total agreement. Even so we sometimes read of some evil-doer and felt almost angry enough to kill. Individual anger we could understand; there was logic in it and there could be justice behind it. But war was a different matter. History showed that greed and the lust for power, camouflaged under the masks of patriotism, religion and honour, had always been the true causes of war. Millions of people were hard at work in factories and arsenals making the means of their own destruction and even fancy uniforms to dress up in for the carnage. The great war machine on which foolish humanity wastes its potential, for the God Profit, has no conscience; but for us humanity had lost its case on war.

War for religion seemed just as illogical. At the risk of my sanity I had often puzzled about how matter of any form had begun. Darwin's great intellect had given us the Origin of the Species, of which Nature showed us many proofs. And he had knocked the man-made idea of a Maker in human form off its false pedestal. Some great Intelligence beyond our grasp may be responsible; just as a white-coated scientist is beyond the conception of the microbes he studies, we are equally out of our depth. Just as children will accept the idea of Father Christmas without questioning how he gets down the chimney, or how he manages to get down millions in a single night, because they love the toys and treats; so we poor bewildered humans accept our many gods. To have no belief is a terrible alternative, but it is better to face up to our ignorance and to stop relying on God for our blessings and blaming the Devil for our ill-fortune, and to start making the most of this incredible experience called life, and helping others to do the same.

The cynicism behind power politics left us disillusioned. We knew that Britain was turning a blind eye to Hitler's atrocities, and actually even helping him by supplying the raw materials for weapons, under the impression and hope that he would attack not us but Russia and its regime hated by the West. But the signs of war were more and more ominous. It seemed now that Hitler was planning conquests East and West. The British public began to decry Hitler and his fascist ally Mussolini. People began to boycott the Italian cafe where I worked. It seemed like an act of fate when we were offered the job of managing a small newsagent's and tobacconist's in Holloway Road. The chief accountant where Syd worked had bought four shops and offered us this chance. Our joint wage would be three pounds a week, about a pound less than we were earning between us but there was much more room and free accommodation. We would not have to spend anything on fares, and we could share the long hours to suit ourselves. We jumped at the chance, and moved in. My younger sister had now left school, and longed to come and live with us and get a job in London. She came and after a couple of weeks holiday, she got a job just down the road in a potted paste factory. She has never eaten potted paste since.

We were going along quite happily, still retaining a slight hope that war might be averted, when on Friday the first of September Hitler invaded Poland. Now there was no hope. Now I had to take my young sister home to the Forest at once, and Syd told me to stay there as well. He was convinced that London would be bombed immediately.

But I could not leave him to cope on his own; up at five thirty sorting out the papers, getting the rounds out, running the shop such long hours, getting his food, doing the minimal housework. Soon I went back to London to be with him again. There were no bombs.

Everything was eerily normal, and people were talking about the Phoney War. If only it had been! Like two dogs that growl and snarl and threaten each other and then walk away! A few months of this unease went by, and then I had a letter from home telling of a job for Syd; in the woods, tree-planting. The pay was poor, but we could have the tiny cottage next to my parents. We told the shop-owner and stayed while he found another young couple, and then back to the peace of the sylvan surroundings of my childhood where we settled in happily in the snug little cottage next to Mam and Dad.

All normal young married women long to have a baby. I was now twenty-five but I was still trying to suppress these feelings. Syd's wages were very small, and this was no world to bring a baby into. But Nature would not be put off. One day I was struck with a terrible nausea; the thought of food, even the simple rationed fare we had, was utterly repugnant, and even tea suddenly tasted like poison. Mam smiled wisely.

"That's morning sickness. You've got a baby on the way, my girl!"

Morning sickness! Morning! This was lasting all day!

I had never felt so ill, even cooking simple potatoes for Syd's tea made me hold my nose. I lost a lot of weight very quickly. Mam cajoled and scolded and coaxed me to get something down, but my taste-buds had gone berserk. All I could fancy to eat were dried porridge oats or oatmeal, and cider to drink — in between taking surreptitious sniffs from the Brasso tin! We now had ration books, and such things as oranges, bananas and imported foods were only a fading memory. After four and a half months the nausea cleared up, though my distaste of normal food lasted right through. But Nature certainly works miracles. Despite her capricious cruelty to my appetite and my innards, I produced a healthy six-pound baby boy.

According to the doctor he was not due for two more weeks. I thought I was prepared! I thought I knew all about the pangs of childbirth! I thought I had made plans to help me through my labour. While in London we had bought for four pounds a good second-hand radiogram and with it a few records. The music from these records used to transport my spirits to a sort of heaven on earth. "Entry of the Queen of Sheba", "Ballet Egyptian", "The Lark" by GalliCurci, "Thieving Magpie", I was going to have this music on while in labour, and Syd promised he would put them on as soon as I started.

When about midnight I began to have severe stomach ache I was not alarmed. The privy was half-way down the garden and it was dark and cold. As I was struggling to put some clothes on, Syd woke up.

"What's the matter, darling?"

"Oh, I've got a terrible belly-ache."

"Is it the baby?"

"No, can't be. It's not due yet, but I must get down to the privy! Oh, God, this pain is terrible."

"Shall I go next door and wake your Mam?"

"No! Oh-oh-oh yes! Please!"

I had got downstairs now, but the pain had made me sink on to my knees. Mam gave one look at me, and said to Syd "Help her back upstairs. Then get on your bike and go for Nurse Williams. And hurry."

It was a two-mile pedal through the dark, and Syd wasted no time getting off. Meanwhile Mam bustled about getting the fire going for boiling the water, and waking up Dad and my sister. Dad came to the bottom of the stairs and called up "Be brave, my wench, you'll soon 'ave a lovely little babby in your arms." It was the only time in my life when I felt I was in a situation beyond his understanding; this agony was woman's own. Mam sent my sister to wake up the village midwife. But I had had our first-born all on my own before they got to me.

When all was eventually calmed down Syd said "We didn't think about playing you any records. D'you want me to go downstairs and put them on for you now?" I shook my head. The six-pound precious bundle in my arms was all I needed!

CHAPTER
NINE

When the time came we had no option with our consciences but to register as conscientious objectors. Syd was willing to volunteer as a stretcher-bearer, but I was opposed to this. I truly believe that when Nation goes to war against Nation it is an obscene indulgence of Man's lowest instincts, although Nature has given him a mind to reason with and a tongue to talk reason. If you are prepared to bomb and shoot and kill people, then your hate must be justified. But if you are taking them prisoner and treating them humanely you cannot hate them. So war becomes a farce.

We were summoned to the tribunal at Bristol. I explained to them how I felt and was unconditionally discharged from war duties. Syd's objection was upheld subject to him being obliged to work only in sawmills for the duration. Brother-in-law Pat was a peace-loving but very practical man. He felt that there were just too many odds stacked against idealism. When he was called up he became a soldier but because of hearing trouble he was posted eventually into clerical duties. He was now a sergeant stationed in Hereford, where he soon found accommodation for his mother, his sister, her baby boy, and for Flo. Flo and he had given up their flat in London, but his mother was keeping hers on. The three women found work, Flo as a grocery shop assistant. She became pregnant but worked till her seventh month when she had premature twins, a boy and a girl, in Hereford hospital. Sadly the little girl only survived for ten days, and she left behind a delicate and very small brother hanging on to life. Pat was sent away, and we all thought it a good idea for Flo to come and live with us, and a good idea it certainly was. I cannot think of a nicer person to live with than Flo, and I loved helping to take care of her baby.

The war dragged on into its fifth year. The general opinion was that it was grinding to a halt. Pat's mother was a hundred per cent Cockney and she was longing to be back in her own cosy flat in Marylebone. The marriage of Pat's sister had broken up; her soldier husband had found someone else. So mother and daughter with the little grandson made up their minds to return to London and live together. There was a lull in the bombing. Soon they wrote to Flo that a three-floored tenement house in Lisson Grove that had been bombed had now been repaired by the government and the six flats were going at a very cheap controlled rent. Did she want one? Flo was a Londoner and had always had the intention of returning. This seemed a good chance and she took it.

I had not foreseen how the loss of her company would hit me. We had become like sisters as well as close friends. Kind, helpful and intelligent, she had enriched my life with her presence. Soon she wrote to us to say there was an empty flat to let on the floor above hers. We decided to take it and follow her. None of us had any idea of the ferocity of the war that was to come before it ended. London was Syd's home, and most of my ten years as domestic servant and waitress had been spent there. We had just enough money to hire an aged driver and his even more aged wagon to take the three of us and our few pieces of furniture back to war-torn London. (We had abandoned our five-bob piano in our first rooms in Maida Vale, courtesy of Mrs Truelove.) With a couple of days to go I was suddenly stricken down with that same never-to-be-forgotten nausea of my first pregnancy, but this time I knew what it was.

Under the grey winter sky war-battered London looked tired and drab, and it seemed that we had come to one of its drabbest corners when the wagon drew up outside the tenement on a corner of Lisson Grove. What misleading names London gives its streets. Grove, indeed! A blade of grass or a tree would have withered and died from a broken heart. I began to have misgivings. What on earth had we done, leaving the Forest of Dean for this? And adjoining the tenement was a side street, two rows of small terraced houses let off into rooms. My heart sank. Then Flo opened the entrance door and I began to feel better. She had the key to our three rooms, and they were a pleasant surprise; two bedrooms and a large kitchen cum diner cum everything else all done out in pale cream. There was a big window in each room and an extra one in the bigger bedroom. The ceilings were high. The kitchen had an open fireplace, and a black iron gas stove was already installed. There was a sink and a cold tap. I knew at once that I could make a home here. There was no bathroom in the tenement, and we would be sharing the toilet on the landing with three other flats. This seemed a small enough matter at the time, and so it was when compared with what was to come.

By now rationing was very severe, but somehow Flo had made a delicious cooked dinner for us and the driver. She must have sacrificed her own precious coupons to do it, and I had brought our rations with me so I could share with her. So we all started to carry our things upstairs, and Chris stood on the pavement to watch. A couple of houses down the street a toddler girl sat on a doorstep eating chips out of newspaper. Our precocious two-and-a-half year old son took the opportunity to go and demand a chip. He got a sharp refusal and a sharp shove-off, but he grabbed a couple and ran back. Flo grabbed him and took him indoors before the child's mother came out to see what she was howling for. Clearly Chris was not intimidated by London, but I was not up to a row with an irritated Cockney neighbour.

Syd soon got a job in a canalside sawmill. Flo's companionship helped me to bear the dreadful early months of pregnancy nausea. The bombing raids became more frequent; the siren's ghastly noise waking us up in the small hours. I used to put Chris to bed on a blanket, with his woolly hat on the pillow, ready to put on; then with the blanket folded round him Syd could carry him to Marylebone station to shelter in the Underground. Even up to eight months pregnant I could still keep up with him and Flo carrying her son Leslie. Sleeping, or trying to sleep, lying on a hard and crowded railway platform was made bearable by the communal spirit that is inspired by shared suffering.

As my time came nearer and nearer I began to dread going into labour during the night and having to face the blacked-out streets and the hellish skies pierced with the red flashes from the anti-aircraft guns. We tried to sleep until the all-clear sounded, and then we staggered home to face another grim day. But there came one night when there was no all-clear. Syd left us at six o'clock in the morning; he had to go to work. Then an air-raid warden came round to tell us there would be no all-clear. Pilotless planes, the famous Flying Bombs, were coming over London all the time. When their engines cut out they and their load of high explosive simply fell on to London's roads and buildings. There was no defence possible; when their engines stopped you just had to dive for cover and hope.

Any shred of courage I had left was soon dissipated by this new threat. Syd insisted, and was adamant, that I take Chris and return once again to the Forest, and there hopefully have the baby in safety. Syd's stepfather had died soon after war had started, and his mother had come to live with us. A widow in her late forties she soon met a hitherto confirmed bachelor in his sixties. They married and she went to live in his cottage at Drybrook, and now Flo and Leslie went to stay with them.

Richard, our second son, duly arrived, and it was all becoming a bit overcrowded for my parents. So when a young woman cousin of mine, living in a primitive cottage at the top of the village, took her two children away to live with friends for the duration, I was glad to rent her place for ten shillings a week.

Poor Syd! Up there in London! Facing the bombs, working very long hours, fire-watching at night at the sawmill, subsisting on starvation rations! He came to see us as often as his job and the money would allow him. Every time he came he made my heart ache. He was getting thinner and thinner and had multiple boils up his arms from lack of proper nourishment. Once again I began to have doubts. After all I had married him for better or for worse, and my place was with him. So I insisted on going back with him to try to live again in London.

Surely the war must end soon! But like a wounded evil dragon in its death throes it became more dangerous than ever. One morning we felt something like a distant earthquake that actually shook the rows of tenement houses. There were no flying bombs about and there had been no warning. The most popular conjecture was that a gas-main had exploded, but we soon learned the truth. Hitler was sending over rockets; they came with such speed that no warning was possible; they could not be seen; they could not be heard until they landed and the lethal load of explosive destroyed people and property. A hunted fox has a chance to run and hope. A mouse can hope for a short while to outwit the teasing killing paws of the cat. All we could do was just wait hopelessly to see if the next rocket had our number on it.

My supreme nightmare at this time was that the children would be buried under rubble, and we would not be able to get to them. This was not helped by the realisation that this was happening to somebody all the time all over London. A few more rockets fell and again it was time for us to think about going back to the Forest. I did not need Syd's urging. Back I went to the empty cottage I had left, and this time to stay until the end of the war in Europe. The relief that the war was really over and that we had survived was almost too wonderful to bear!

The long years of deprivation, hunger and killing were all over, and, as we thought, for evermore. Now began the happy years of peace and reconstruction. At this stage I always think of two men I never met but whose memory I shall respect and love as long as I live; Clement Attlee and Stafford Cripps, our post-war Prime Minister and his Chancellor; two highly intelligent men of great humanity who set about improving the lot of the masses. Trying to feed our children properly on painfully inadequate rations had meant that Syd and I went hungry often. The rich had always been all right; there was a flourishing black market for them. Now there was cheap food at controlled prices, and generous rations for it. This was our priority import from the Commonwealth. Many other items such as furniture, all of good quality, were sold under the cheap controlled utility scheme. I have a utility tallboy, still in use and sound as a bell after forty-five years. The "I'm alright, Jack" greedy opportunist entrepreneurs were severely discouraged, while even clothing and other necessities went on a price-controlled ration.

Syd's wages were low even when augmented by my

few hours work as a charwoman. Yet we could all have full bellies. Priority for the construction industry was the building of houses and flats for the working people. "Big Business" and the City were not amused, but the Government persevered and put Britain back on its feet.

We settled down to the task of raising our growing family. We were too busy to speculate on what might have been or on what was to come. It was a time of great joy and of unbearable sorrow, as I have written in my book *Back to the Forest*. Ten years later, with another son and a six-year-old daughter, we went back again to the Forest, this time for good. We lived for twenty-five years in a tied cottage in the heart of the pastoral beauty of a country estate where we brought up our family and saw them all married with children of their own.

CHAPTER
TEN

After twenty-five years in the tied cottage that we had moved into from London, Syd's retirement was drawing very near. Now we had the problem of what we were going to do and where we were going to go when the time came for us to leave. But this was solved for us by a miraculous turning-point in our lives. When I was sixty I had tried to write about the old times in the Forest, and I found that I had enough talent to write my auto-biography. It became a minor best-seller, broadcast three times on the radio, and two extracts were taken to be used on television. So, with our son Chris acting as guarantor for a modest bank loan, my earnings bought us a tiny cottage with a good-sized garden in a delightful hamlet called Cliffords Mesne only four miles as the crows fly from our tied cottage. By the time that Syd retired it was repaired and modernised to council standards. And then came the trauma of moving.

"I 'ouldn't try to move thic 'un, Missus. 'Im 'a' bin there too long. The roots be settled too deep in the ground."

An old countryman friend was with me in the cottage yard. Time and circumstances were obliging us to move, and I was contemplating taking the old clematis for the new garden. I was attached to that clematis. For twenty years it had festooned one of our walls with its profusion of purple blooms, a gift from a friend to help us settle in a tied cottage. Unlike the clematis I could walk to the new and probably last chapter in my destiny. But I had been there five years longer than that clematis. I too had put down roots; roots of emotion that wanted to cling to my old habitat. At sixty-four years old, in horticultural terms, I was too old for transplanting from my familiar plot.

A theory is now expounded by scientists that plants can not only feel but can actually make sounds although they are inaudible to the human ear. Should this be proven it will be enough to drive the poor vegetarians bonkers. The idea horrifies me. Who would then want to cut the heart out of a cabbage or tear a lettuce limb from limb? And imagine the agony of the spuds when they come to the boil!

Yet sadly vegetation does die in drought or darkness, and like old people when they are uprooted, mature shrubs will often wither and die in new soil. Seedlings, like babies whose limbs are still to grow, will adapt themselves in suitable conditions. I left the clematis, but with Syd, my husband, the trunk around which I had clung and bloomed, moved the five miles to our new abode.

I really did not have a lot to moan about. For one thing, it was ours; my writing earnings had enabled us to buy it. Humble and tiny (it had been sold to the previous buyer eighty years before for fifty pounds) it had three precious assets: a good-sized garden, an open fire, and beautiful pastoral surroundings, and it was set in the charming hamlet of Cliffords Mesne. Here on gentle slopes surrounded by woodlands and fields sit a number of old stone cottages and farmhouses, and a few fine big houses, not quite castles perhaps but miniature manors set in delightful gardens. We have a pub, a phone-box by a tiny green, a little church and an old village school transformed into a tiny village hall. But there is no shop or post office, and the bus runs twice a week. Our cottage, probably the smallest in the hamlet, straggles with four others up a steep and narrow side road which peters out into one of the hedgerowed lanes and public paths that criss-cross all about.

We soon discovered that we have lovely neighbours. The old couple in the cottage below are kindness itself and spare me the surplus new-laid eggs from their few hens. The old husband is forever active as though challenging the grave, but the wife, in her late seventies, is too old for country walks.

But Ivy, from the cottage at the top of the row, young and spry for her seventy-two years and a country-lover, likes the activity, and before Syd retired took me with her most afternoons. I love to call for her after lunch and stand at their garden gate to admire the flower-bordered path to the door, the neat rows of vegetables, the fruit trees and shrubs. The cat suns itself on the window sill, and Lucy, their little mongrel dog, comes trotting up to meet me, tail wagging in anticipation of her walk. The cottage, a small gem once thatched, is still the sort of place one would expect Little Grey Rabbit to emerge from, and cosy plump Ivy puts me in mind of her. Stan, her husband, cannot come. Long years of working in the painting and decorating trade have left him with an ulcer and severe bronchial asthma. He needs all his breath and fading stamina for his beloved garden.

Ivy brings a bag and on the way to the woods we gather choice herbage from the hedgerows, and she always carries sugar lumps in her pocket. She misses nothing and takes an infectious pleasure from every newly-opened wild flower, calling them sweet country names: Welsh bells, jack-in-the-hedge.

Where most animals are concerned I am a coward and I envy her approach to all living creatures. I stand well back when we come to old Duke the stallion tethered in a grassy clearing in the woods. As casually as Barbara Woodhouse she feeds him a sugar lump and a handful of herbage. Then, a little distance away, we pay a social call on a couple of billy goats to give them their share.

In their seasons we stand in homage to Nature admiring the drifts of wild daffodils, bluebells and fox-gloves, and keep an eye on the wild orchids she has spotted. She pauses a minute, sniffing. "Smell that fox?" she asks. But I cannot. When we get to the crest of the woods the panoramic views of rural England give us a good reason to pause and rest our old legs. "Can you understand it, Win," she asks, "that they can even talk about such things as nuclear war?" The soft winds in the trees echo our sighs.

One of the ten children of a gamekeeper, Ivy, like me, has known frugality and poverty. So we never return home empty-handed. We carry our booty, perhaps a bundle of kindling wood, or blackberries, sloes and rosehips from the hedges. Sometimes I take a bucket and shovel, for horseriders abound hereabout. We make it a round trip home, passing a couple of caravans in a field, where a bevy of about eight dogs of mixed pedigree rush about barking to inspect us. The first time this happened I took to my heels, but Ivy greets them all with a few words and they stand curious and polite to let us pass.

Before we moved in, when Syd and I used to come over to work on the cottage in our spare time, we sometimes passed a pony and trap driven by a woman of extraordinary good looks, a model I thought, for Queen Boadicea. Her long black hair was brushed back from a face that would make a sculptor long for his clay, or an artist for his easel and brushes. It was she and her husband and children who lived in the caravans and owned the goats, old Duke, the dogs and the mares in the field.

Some years ago, when she was a teenage girl, this beauty had come with her itinerant family to pitch their homes temporarily on the common behind the church. They had stayed long enough for a local young man's admiration to turn to love. When they moved on he sought her out and eventually won her for his wife.

Now they live surely as Nature intended; they breed those noble equine creatures, they gather the fruits from their orchard, giving to and taking from the earth. In spring, Duke their stallion is tethered on the little common opposite our cottage for the annual ritual of his malehood with the young mares. Wild bluebells and garlic, new green ferns and the shifting shade of the birches provide a romantic bower for their nuptials.

98

I enjoyed seven years of friendship with Ivy. She was a character without envy or spite, and too much of a Nature's lady to recognise social divisions. On her walks through the village and its lanes and by-ways she chatted with everyone she met. Alas, as her seventy-sixth birthday approached, Ivy began to find walking difficult. She was losing her balance from giddy turns until even a stroll around her own garden was too much. Then she had a major stroke. I was at her bedside with one of her two daughters on the other side. "I shall have to take things easier when I get better, Win" she sighed as I held her hand. Then her head fell back on the pillow and I knew she was gone.

The village church was packed for her funeral. "We have lost the village mother", someone remarked. I was only a few years younger than Ivy, but she had mothered me too.

CHAPTER
ELEVEN

I was busy in our back garden when the old widower farmer who owns the fields adjoining popped his head over the hedge. No pot-bellied red-faced figure of legend he, but a streak of sinew seventy-nine years old. He has too much to do to take account of age. He loves and respects his land like a dutiful son.

"The land'll work for you, Missus, if you works for the land. You can't fool Nature, try it and 'er'll 'ave 'er own back on you. Spread plenty o' muck, I say. T'is too much artificials these days. Quick and easy they do want it, but it don't pay in the long run."

He bemoans the passing of the carthorses and leaves the driving of the tractor and such contraptions to his grandson. He heaved a carrier bag over the hedge.

"'Ere's a few pears for you to try, Missus. My old lady used to peel 'em and core 'em, cut 'em in 'alf and cover 'em wi' water and brown sugar wi' a sprinkling o'cloves, and cook 'em in the oven. Puttin' taters in, be you? Well, cut the big 'uns in 'alf on the slope a bit, Missus; you'll get a better crop that way."

I thanked him warmly for the pears and the advice, and commented on the lushness of his meadows.

"Aye, the cows'll 'ave summat good to bite on there. I shall let 'em in tomorrow."

I like cows, gentle creatures, adding an aura of peace to the pastoral scene. Unlike men, they do not argue over the best bit of pasture, nor even argue at all, obliging each other's itches with friendly rubs of the head. They must be slaughtered, but I wish the humane stunning could be done in the field. As a child I once saw a reluctant cow being driven into a slaughterhouse. It knew where it was going, and its piteous mooing still rings in my ears and its efforts to hold back linger in the memory.

When I did my weekly bake, I put a cake in a plastic box to set down by the farmer's door. I knew he was a busy man, and I did not think he would see me. But I was surprised to have the privilege of being asked to step inside. It was a step back sixty years: the big black iron grate, the steel fender and fire-irons, the old fashioned sofa against the wall opposite the window, the wooden chairs and scrubbed top-table. "Oh, I do love that old grate!" I cried, remembering the hours in my childhood when I had toasted myself on the corner of just such a fender as I listened to my old great-aunt and her cronies talking of the past.

"Aye, but 'im's greedy wi' the coal. I 'a' bin thinkin' o' taking 'im out, and 'avin' one o' them Aggros in."

But the way he looked at that old grate belied his words. He had warmed his cold limbs too often by it, had eaten his spiced pears and roast rabbits from its oven, toasted his mother's bread made in the bake-oven by its side, and napped away his weariness before its cosy glow.

No, I thought, you will be carried out of here before that grate is.

"I expect this farmhouse is pretty old?" I ventured.

"Well, I dunno," he said, "nothing round 'ere is all that old. At one time the land from 'ere to Newent, two and a half mile away, was nothing but rough common land. My grandad could remember when tinker folk used to come through 'ere carryin' their 'omes on their backs like snails, anything they could pitch for a bit o' shelter while they tried to get work on the land. Now an' then a family would decide to stay, an' they'd rummage around for summat to build a more substantial place. In time they got stone from the quarries, limbs from the trees, an' built cottages, like that 'un o' yourn. 'Twas all put a stop to, o' course, when the Land Enclosure Act come in."

There must be gypsy blood in me; I could visualise the hardships these families endured. But what a sense of achievement for men and women to start from scratch and fashion a shelter for their family, to wrench a garden from scrubland, and to fence in some ground for an animal or two and some fowls; a more gratifying option than mortgaging your wages for twenty-five years to own a central-heated cubist brick box of a house identical to all those around, and unstamped by an iota of the owner's personality or sweat.

"Mind you," the old man went on, "twenty-five year ago we didn't 'ave the 'lectric nor running water around 'ere. Folks wi' wells in their garden 'ad to let their neighbours come in certain times o' day to get their water. Most people baked their own bread, kept a pig in the sty, and worked their gardens to the last inch. 'Twas paraffin lamps and candles, no television, and people relied on each other for help and company. There was a better spirit about. Aye. Now, today when the 'lectric's cut off, some o' the women do run around like a hen wi' 'er 'ead cut off. I've kept my lamps and a can o' paraffin 'andy."

I remembered his words a few months later when the arctic winter of 1982 fell upon us. I was caught out. Crashing trees brought down the electricity cables, the pump that brings our tap water stopped functioning, our car was marooned by the gate in a snowdrift, and the roads were all made impassable overnight. No light, no cooker, no water, no TV to distract us, only two little stumps of candle in the cottage, and not much bread!

We took stock. Not too bad. We had a small amount of groceries in the cupboard and some home-grown fruit and vegetables in the freezer. We could stick it out for a few days. My saucepans, filled with melting snow and balanced somehow on the open fire, went into mourning, but we made our tea, boiled an egg each, and contrived a bit of stew. Too cold to go to bed we huddled in the dark around the fire.

After three days the real crisis point arrived. Syd was down to his last shreds of tobacco, and I had only enough left for a couple of roll-ups. I have ambivalent feelings for Sir Walter Raleigh. He has my blessings for bringing the potato to Britain, and my frequent curses for doing likewise with tobacco. Syd has been addicted to his pipe since a lad. It always brought him such solace that, some years ago when I was going through a period of overwork and worry when the children were in their teens, he bought me a packet of cigarettes from his parsimonious pocket money.

"Have one when the kids have gone to bed; it'll relax you, darling."

All the scaring propaganda about cancer and heart trouble was still to come. All the same I was forty years old and should have known better. Now, like Syd, puffing nicotine helps me bear the slings and arrows of outrageous fortune; I am hooked. Without it the dark side of our natures comes to the fore. Without his pipe Syd's temper is on a very short fuse, and I revert to irritability and near-manic depression. I could see the headlines: "Elderly couple in double murder in snowbound cottage. No outsiders involved."

Something had to be done. "I'm going to walk to Newent," said Syd, "to get some 'bacca, and anything else you want."

We wanted plenty; I felt guilty at my lack of housewifely foresight. "I'll come with you and help you carry things," I insisted.

It is only five miles there and back to the little country town of Newent. We put on our wellingtons, woolly hats, scarves and warm coats. I girded up my surgical corset. It's a handicap to walking. Without it the dodgy discs in my arthritic spine can come out and I should be a stranded cripple. Laced up tight it hinders the circulation in my elderly legs. My progress is slow at the best of times. Now, with snowdrifts and icy patches to negotiate, and feet made clumsier in wellingtons, it was a crawl but the struggle soon made me rosily warm.

As we walked between the snow-laden hedges it was hard to believe that in a few months the "pick your own fruit and veg" notices would be out at the entrances of the smallholdings on the way. In summer these fruit farms are veritable gardens of Eden: huge areas of neat rows of strawberries with the fat pink fruits peeping between the leaves, gooseberry bushes dripping with their emerald globes, jewel-red raspberries trained up frames, black and red currants. The abundance is marvellous. Then come the apples, millions of them, red, gold and green, on the trees and underneath after a summer gale. Not a snake in sight!

It's a long lane that has no turning, and every turn in the one we struggled through was an achievement, until at last we came to the long straight of Watery Lane with Newent in sight. A nice little country town is Newent, its heart retaining a Tudor flavour with the ancient oak-pillared Market House and timbered black and white buildings, a family town where shoppers and shop-keepers are well acquainted. It is now circled by private and council housing estates, and earlier worms than us had bought up every loaf and candle in the place. But we filled our bags with groceries, bought our tobacco, and made for home.

It was not so bad sitting in the dark, toasting our last few slices on the fire, with some soothing noxious weed to puff. The early night was upon us and the incredible cold creeping in when presently we heard laughter and a dog barking and a knock at the door. Spencer, our grandson, hugging a loaf of bread, came in, followed by our daughter Jenny with two bottles of milk and their little dog.

"We brought it down on my sledge," said Spencer proudly. "We took it down to the shop in Longhope first, and they let us have two loaves and four bottles of milk."

Now the Longhope shop is at least two and a half miles down a steep hill from their cottage almost on the crest, and our place is about the same distance down the other side. Our daughter and grandson had taken on a ten-mile journey, slithering and slipping over the ice and through the drifts to bring us bread and milk! What hugs and kisses they got, as well as some tinned soup hotted up on the fire!

Later on Syd said to me, "Reckon we could be in for another spell like nineteen-forty-seven. That started just like this lot, and about the same time. Let's hope not." His words, and the cramping cold, and the deep snow outside, brought it all back so vividly, and I was glad that I was not sitting there by the meagre firelight on my own. I shuddered as I recalled the shock I had suffered to my disbelief in the supernatural.

At the time we were living in a tenement house in Lisson Grove. The arctic weather had temporarily closed down the sawmill where Syd worked. This was a blow to our shoestring finances, so I was delighted when Meg, who lived underneath us, said she could get me an early morning charring job. It would be in the house next door to her job in Wimpole Street. It would mean getting up at half-past five, walking to work, and cleaning the rooms before the consultants came. The owner of the house, a famous surgeon, lived in the top-floor flat, and let the spare rooms to other consultants.

At quarter-past five the next morning, leaving our warm bed to dress in the shivering cold, I regretted my promise as I tiptoed down the stairs to Meg's door. Quietly we shut the front door and stepped out into the frozen street, out into a London with hardly a soul about. After a few minutes of hurrying we were as warm as toast and this unfamiliar sleeping London seemed quite wonderful. My ring at the basement door was answered by the dressing-gowned wife of my employer. She was a nice, friendly lady, and showed me where the hoover and cleaning things were kept, and the rooms and the hall to clean. I would get some breakfast later, when the cook got up. Then she took herself back to bed.

Soon it was nine o'clock, and I had eaten some breakfast in the basement kitchen. Now I had the dentist's rooms to do. These rooms were in an annexe built on to the back of the house, on what had been a garden. The house had central heating, and I was warm from my labours, yet as soon as I stepped through the door of the annexe corridor, a chill shiver went right through me; a shiver more of fright than cold. The consulting rooms were furnished much to my taste: fat comfortable tapestry-covered armchairs by a lovely fireplace, curtains to match, other pieces of beautiful furniture, and bowls of flowers. I could not imagine anything more welcoming. So why then did I feel as though the hairs on the back of my neck were standing up, and why was this terrible feeling of dread overcoming me, even as the winter sunshine was actually coming through the window?

The next room was the dentist's surgery, very clinically up to date, all white with touches of blue. I have a paranoid fear of the dentist's chair, because I have a blood problem and need stitches after every extraction. But would that account for my peculiar reaction, I thought, as I cleaned the rooms with more speed than conscientiousness? It was all too absurd to mention to anybody. I would forget it.

But the next morning it happened again just the same, and the horror never diminished while I cleaned those annexe rooms during the two weeks I worked there.

Some thirty years later I was sitting by the fireside and reading through a Sunday colour supplement. There was an article in it about the nefarious activities of Burke and Hare, the body snatchers, who took the corpses to the back door of a Wimpole Street house through the garden for illegal dissection by curious surgeons. And, I read, when short of stock this pair would "finish off" vagrants to get more money.

The number of the house was the one I had worked in!

The dentist's rooms had been built on the site of the back garden.

But I still don't really believe in the supernatural. Though sometimes I am tempted to think the wraith of early morning mist in Bill's field the other side of our garden hedge is the spirit of Bill. He struggled on into his eighties before his emaciated earth-encrusted hands could no longer hang on to his beloved land. He has gone, but his old black grate remains.

108

CHAPTER
TWELVE

One thing about achieving a bit of fame as a writer, one never knows who will come knocking at the door. I felt flattered that people wanted to meet me but sometimes it was inconvenient when they caught me in the late morning with my teeth out and my hair in curlers. I dodge early rising whenever I can; a sort of backlash from my days as a domestic servant when I had to be up at six. I cannot ride a bike or drive a car, so there was no dodging them by going out, and I loved using all my spare time working in the garden. Syd still had a couple of years before retiring.

Probably because we were past sixty before we acquired the luxury of a telephone, the adrenalin was still taking off when I heard it ringing. This was because of the occasional exciting voice at the other end, for example one of those charming BBC ones. This time it was a lady asking me to take part in a TV book programme transmitted at eleven o'clock on a Sunday evening. My first reaction was panic and polite refusal. I had a good excuse: it would be too late for me. I could not get back from London at that time to be up in the morning to send Syd off to his work at the sawmill. (This was before he had retired.) Not to worry, she reassured me, the programme was recorded in the afternoon and sent out later. By now the old ego had perked up and I accepted. Then I sat down for an attack of the flutters.

I had only a couple of days' notice to pull my nerves together. Being a plain nondescript old woman beyond the help of cosmetics I did not have to worry too much about my appearance. I had a nice new blouse, but my hair would need a trim-up. For thirty years I had been cutting my Syd's hair. There is not much left to cut now, hardly enough to give him a ruffle. He returns the compliment. I manage the side bits myself and frizz them out a bit using a few of his pipe cleaners for curlers, and he cuts the back for me.

"Make a proper job of it this time," I told him. In the summer we sit on chairs in the garden, but this was winter, so I drew up my chair by the fire and put a towel round my shoulders. There is nothing I find so soothing and relaxing as having my hair combed and brushed. It was a good blazing fire. My chin went down, and I felt deliciously drowsy as he combed, brushed and snipped away with scissors and clippers. I must have nodded off.

His voice sounded a bit apprehensive when he poked me awake saying, "There you are; I've done the best I can with it," and made a strategic escape into the lavatory. I realised why when I stood up and looked with the aid of a hand-mirror in the looking glass at what he had done to the back of my head. Trying to achieve a straight edge he had cut and clipped my hair practically bald at the back to the level of my ears and then he had given up in despair.

"I didn't ask you to turn me into a bloody Mohican,"

I shouted at him through the lavatory door. "Just you wait till you come out!" I wailed. I'll have my own back, I thought angrily. When I cut his hair next time I'll cut off the bits he lets grow long at the sides to comb over his bald patch!

We had arranged for our married daughter to drive me up to Lime Grove. When she came to pick me up she gave a little shriek of horror at my haircut.

"It's your Dad," I moaned, "look what he did to it."

Ever loyal to her beloved dad she gave me little sympathy. "Serves you right, Mummy. You could have gone to the hairdressers for once."

My confidence had a little boost when we reached the studios and a friendly commissionaire showed us our reserved parking space. We were half an hour early. Jenny looked at me.

"You look shattered, Mummy. Come on, we'll find somewhere where you can have a little drop of brandy."

We found a pub, and a dingy insalubrious place it was, and obviously not the sort of place frequented by women at this time of day. The few customers, all men, eyed us with curiosity — well, eyed Jenny at least. I often wonder how someone like me could produce this tall beautiful girl; no doubt her tall handsome dad had a lot to do with it. We kept our eyes down while Jenny drank her tonic water and I the unfamiliar double brandy; then back to Lime Grove Studios, and just in time.

Holding my head well back, chin high, trying to hide Syd's haircut, I must have looked a lot more confident than I felt when we were shown into the reception room. They are a lot of charmers at the BBC. It was nice being introduced to the programme planners and the famous compère.

Presently an attractive middle-aged lady came up, put her hands on my shoulders, and said, "Hello, old butty, I've been *so* looking forward to meeting you!" It was Edna Healey, then of number eleven Downing Street. This friendly greeting in the dialect of the Forest of my youth, which was her birthplace too, calmed my nerves quite a bit; but not enough to eat much of the excellent cold buffet laid on. I drank the proffered glass of sherry, and as this mixed up with the brandy I began to feel quite flushed.

With Edna Healey on the interviewing panel were a glamorous coloured cabaret artiste and a newspaper editor. The interviewees were a famous elderly author, some other well-known erudite gentlemen, and myself. The ceiling of the studio was almost covered with mechanical appliances. Cameramen and technicians were thick on the ground. A clear space on the floor held chairs for the panel, a desk and seat for the compère, and a chair for the interviewees. Despite all the paraphernalia it seemed quite inconceivable that what was taking place could be seen at the flick of a switch in viewers' homes all over England. The programme went without a hitch, no retakes necessary.

Obviously I had not been the only one feeling tense; everyone's mood now seemed much more relaxed. After some friendly chat with some of the other participants I looked round for Jenny. She and Mrs Healey were talking together.

It was a bit of a bombshell when Mrs Healey said,

"Now, Winnie, I've been persuading Jenny to bring you round to eleven Downing Street for a drink. I'd so love to have a chat with you." I already felt a bit like Cinderella who had gone to the ball; no doubt the paucity of my social life made me unduly impressed. I politely demurred, telling her we were going on to visit a sister and brother-in-law before going home.

"Oh, but you can still come along afterwards." Jenny agreed, and told her the number and type of her car so that Mrs Healey could tell the policemen on duty to let us through.

Seated in a posh armchair in the grandeur of Downing Street and talking with this interesting, charming lady, with yet another drink in my hand, I grinned to myself as I thought that not so long ago I had been thankful to scrub floors in London for a few shillings to augment Syd's modest wages. When requested to do so by Mrs Healey I signed the Visitors' Book in the entrance hall with quite a flourish!

When I got home Syd was preparing for bed; he had to be up at six to go to work in the sawmill. But our eldest son, Chris, was there.

"Come on, Mum," he said, "I'll take you to our house to see yourself on our colour telly." So I did, and I was thankful that the camera had not focused on the back of my head.

It was the early hours of the morning when I came home and snuggled down by the sleeping Syd. I felt that I had had quite a day!

Three years after we had moved Syd retired. He was just

over sixty-five and I was nearly sixty-eight. It took a long time to get used to the idea that we were free to go out during the week. Syd had always worked on Saturday mornings. Saturday afternoons we did our shopping. Sundays were for family and gardening. Now I began to think of outings just for pleasure. We had a calendar on the wall with a picture of Lower Slaughter in the Cotswolds. "That's where we'll go," said Syd, tapping the calendar, "into the Cotswolds and have a look at that place."

What a debt we owe to the stonemasons of the past for building those gems of honey-coloured cottages, houses and manors that add such beauty to the gentle undulating pastoral landscape of the Cotswolds! And also to our humble forebears who constructed theirs of oak and wattle and daub.

"Oh, let's stop here and have a walk around!" I cried as we came through a vale where an urgent stream splashed along beside the road. On one side flat pastures stretched away into a green mist and on the other rose a gentle hill of fields dotted with trees, and on each side of the road were some ancient cottages and gardens.

One tiny Tudor specimen seemed to have come right from an illustration in a fairy tale. "Oh, just look!" I cried out with pleasure, "the little crooked house!"

"And there," said Syd as we approached, "is the little crooked man to go with it." Each wall of the cottage seemed to have settled on to its earthy foundation independently, leaving the thatched roof to accommodate them as best it may. Storms and sun had rusted and bleached the thatch to a gentle mixture of hues that

114

matched the battered old trilby on the man's head, hat and head obviously weathering the seasons of many years. The bones of his old frame contending with the ravages of time had like the cottage bent and twisted, but not too much to keep him off his garden where he was now busy with his hoe. We looked over his neat hedge and he returned our gaze with friendly interest.

"That's a beautiful specimen you've got there," said Syd admiring an old-fashioned rose covered with pink blossoms by the side of the cottage.

"Aye. That's me wife's. 'Er planted that 'un. 'Er 'a' bin up in the churchyard a few years now, but I do pick a bunch an' take up to 'er reg'lar as long as they do last."

"And what a magnificent hydrangea over there coming out early," enthused Syd.

"Step on in a minute, an' 'ave a look at 'n," the old man offered, opening the gate. "That'n is me Lady Millicent." He automatically touched his hat as he said the name. "'Er *was* a lady, by name an' by nature. Used to talk to the workpeople as though they were 'uman bein's like 'erself. Not like 'is Nibs. I was workin' by the Big House, repairin' a greenhouse, an' 'er come by. Real friendly an' nice 'er was. I told 'er what a picture 'er garden looked, especially the hyder-rangers, so she took me off a slip there an' then wi' 'er own 'ands. 'Take this,' 'er said, 'an' if it doesn't root you ask the head gardener to give you another slip.' I do allus put the first flowers off it on 'er grave, on the quiet like, but I 'ouldn't put a bunch o' dandelions on 'is Nibs.

"I bain't no scholar, come out o' school when I was twelve when me dad died and I started work on the estate. But though 'is Nibs went to Eton an' Cambridge an' all over the world for his education, 'e couldn't so much as take the measurements of a window. Wasn't much of a husband to 'er Ladyship, more for his fancy women an 'oppin' up to London, but when 'er died it must 'ave affected 'is 'ead. Wouldn't live in the Big House any more, turned it over to 'is daughter, an' moved into the gatehouse. A queer move for an aristocrat like 'im; like movin' from a cider barrel to a thimble; but 'e wanted some big pieces o' furniture put in there from *'is* rooms at the Manor. People do reckon this gatehouse is summat special as 'twas built by Indigo something or other and tourists be allus gawpin' at it an' takin' photos. But it's a awkward place inside for a removal man; the stairs be full of twists. Anyway the great wardrobe 'e wanted wouldn't go up they stairs nohow. Then it must go through the upstairs window, says 'is Nibs. I was workin' on the estate then wi' the maintenance man. 'I don't think the aperture is big enough, Sir,' 'e says. 'Oh, yes, it is, I have measured it. Take out the window frame but don't touch the stonework. I want it done on Monday morning. Get the block and tackle ready and I'll come personally to see the wardrobe hoisted in.' 'Yes, sir,' 'an' when the Squire was out o' sight 'and no, sir. I can tell wi' me eye that wardrobe won't go through that window, but come on, we'll measure it ourselves — the sill will 'ave to come out whatever 'is Nibs says, the aperture's inch an' 'alf short.'

"With the help of some other estate workers we 'ad the wardrobe under the window an' the 'oist ready by the time 'is Lordship 'usted up, an' there the bugger still 'ung outside that window whilst we men tried to do the impossible an' manoeuvre it inside. 'Is Nibs got proper rattled but 'e'd said it'd go in, an' go in it 'ad to 'cos 'e wasn't goin' to admit 'e was wrong. Suddenly 'e remembered a pressing engagement. 'I'll have to leave you men to get it in. I've an appointment to keep,' an' off 'e went. 'Twas an awkward predicament for the maintenance man. The wardrobe 'ad to be got in, but the stonework wasn't to be disturbed. 'Bugger the old fool', 'e said, an' 'e got 'is 'ammer an' chisel an' sweated 'is guts out takin' the heavy stone sill out. We got the wardrobe in, an' mixed up some mortar to set the sill back in. 'E made a good job on it but anyone wi' one eye could see it 'ad bin tinkered wit' 'Ah, I see you managed it, Barnes; I told you it could be done,' bragged 'is Nibs. And of course you didn't argyfy wi' the Squire them days.

"'Is old man was still alive then, an' 'e was a bad 'un; like father, like son. When the old man got crippled up in a wheelchair 'e still wanted to go potting 'is pheasants though 'e was nearly blind an' couldn't 'a shot a elephant at twenty yards, not to be sure. But gamekeeper 'ad to fix a special shoot day just for the old man. They 'ad a job I can tell you gettin' 'im in 'is wheelchair to the top of the steep 'ill an' parkin' 'im on a bit o' level by the big wood where the pheasants be bred. There 'im would sit whilst the beaters went into the copse an' sent the birds over. The old man'd shoot at the sky while everybody kep' well clear, an' though 'e never 'it a bird only by accident, 'e'd still tell the keeper as 'e'd fetched a dozen birds down, an' to pick 'em up an' bring 'em down to the Manor kitchens. Then keeper an' 'is lad 'ad to scour the wood an' a dozen shot pheasants 'ad to be got some'ow an' took to the kitchen. But as I said nobody argyfied wi' gentry them days."

Suddenly he finished gazing back across the years and his eyes fell again on his garden. Syd was full of envy for his neat rows of prolific vegetables, and said so. "Well, o' course, 'tis manure," said the old gardener. "I be very lucky wi' manure; just got to go through the gate at the bottom o' me garden into the fields for sheep's droppin's, cow-pats, an' hosses' leavin's. You do want a good mixture o' manures and compost, then you can forget all them fancy packets o' fertilisers." Looking at his lush garden, I would not have dreamed of argyfying with him.

As we walked around the back of the cottage I could not resist peeping through the window into the low-ceilinged living room. It was dark, cosy and primitively furnished; I would not have been surprised to see Mole, Ratty and Badger sitting round the fireplace discussing the problems of Toad's outrageous behaviour. Thanking the old man for sparing us his time and advice we went back to the car and headed for Lower Slaughter.

Reality has a knack of taking the edge off coloured pictures. When you arrive the grass is never that green, the roses not so red. The placid blue water has turned into a grey torrent, the cloudless sky has become a drizzling slate roof. The hill has shrunk and the castle diminished. The gardens are weedy, the lawns need mowing, the charming inn is closed. The sunlit sandy beach is a strand of painful pebbles. So we had looked on our calendar picture with some cynicism.

But this time how wrong we were! Lower Slaughter was even better, much better than the pretty picture on our calendar: nothing from a camera lens could do justice to this gem of rural England. The ugly name conjures up one Todd of barber-shop infamy, but nothing could be more remote from violence than this small settlement built each side of the narrow, sweetly-named Windrush river. A landscape genius could not have planned a river, cottages, trees, greensward, church and manor house into a more serene rustic oasis.

When we arrived one artist was already busy at his easel set up on the grass verge of the little river, trying to capture on his canvas the stone tints of the cottages opposite, and the old watermill at the end of them. Before we settled ourselves down we strolled along the tree-lined road and stared with envy at a house whose garden wall enclosed a stretch of the river. Then at the other side we craned our necks over the wall of a fine old Cotswold manor set in its own spacious grounds. Hard by, a local man stood near the ancient churchyard lychgate and he willingly chatted to us with pride about the thirteenth century church, and urged us to have a look round before we left.

As we passed a row of rose-festooned cottages I could not resist peeping in through the windows to see if they were as enchanting inside as out. Syd poked me along, chastening my invasion of people's privacy. "Well," I remonstrated "what can they expect if they choose to live in such an idyllic place?" By lunch-time the place was crowded with sightseers and there were two more artists busy at their easels. We had claimed our little patch of grass by the river, we had our sandwiches and flasks and the car was parked within sight. We were more than content. I would have liked to emulate some of the children who sat on the low stone wall and dangled their feet in the shallow crystal-clear waters of the Windrush. The tranquil loveliness of the place seemed to imbue children as well as adults; there was no shouting or rough play. People just sat in the sun or strolled up and down, struck like us with a sort of reverence by this perfect summer day in this little Eden.

Before going home we walked down a long lane through farmlands, and then round behind the village to some new houses. Though built of manufactured stone, their sympathetic architecture, their well-kept gardens and the complete lack of garish ostentation, made us forgive the lucky rich who lived there.

When we got home we found a note pushed under our door by some disappointed visitors. Unrepentant, we thought what a pity they too had not gone for a drive into the Cotswolds instead.

"That was lovely," said Syd, "we'll have some more outings like that. There's Bourton-on-the-Water, Stow-on-the-Wold, and there's Cranham. I've been told that's very beautiful. Let's go to Cranham next."

Mention Cranham and I think of porridge.

Long ago when we were children, in that era of poverty and malnutrition, tuberculosis and chest troubles were rife in youngsters. The best-known cure was fresh air and good plain food, and plenty of both. Sanatoriums were built on suitable sites, and my eldest sister spent a period in one at Cranham when she was a toddler. When our thin chesty little brother was four, the doctor decided that he needed a spell there too. He was our adored little brother, the only surviving boy of the three that Mother had borne.

Transport to Cranham was not available except if parents clubbed together to pay for a conveyance to take them. The pits were on short time, two or three shifts a week, and although Mam and Dad scrimped enough to go and see him once, there was simply not enough money in our household for me and my sister to go. We missed him terribly, especially at night, snuggling down between us in the iron bedstead the three of us shared. And often our dad would wistfully ask Mother, "I wonder what our little boy be doin' now at Cranham?" Then at long last a letter came from the authorities. He was coming home from Cranham! In a car! Well not quite to home, because the car could not get up the steep and rutted track to our cottage near the top of the village.

The great day came and Mam and the baby and my sister and I were down at the bottom of the village well before he was due. How my heart pounded with excitement when at last we saw a little black car coming down the main road. He had certainly come home in style.

But who was this miniature aristocrat the man was handing out? Plump, suntanned, incredibly clean, with shining cropped hair, smartly dressed and with a new accent to match! I felt too plebeian and too shy to lavish upon him all my saved-up hugs and kisses. Mam held his hand and set off up the hill, my sister carried the baby and we walked behind, an adoring and humble retinue. When Dad came home from the pit he showed no such reticence. In his pit dirt and despite Mam's reproof he picked up his little boy and hugged him as though he would never let him go.

When bedtime came I squeezed up to the wall on my side and my sister stayed on the edge on her side, to give him the lion's share of our iron bedstead. He wriggled down comfortably between us. "Shall I sing you a song I know?" he asked politely in his strange accent. This would be a privilege. "Oh, yes, please," we enthused.

It was a ribald little ditty and we were quite shocked; our little changeling was coming back down to earth.

"Whatever did the Matron say when she heard you singing that?"

"Oh, I didn't sing it to *her*; only to the maids. I didn't like the matron. She was too strict. One morning I felt sick, and I couldn't eat my porridge. She *made* me eat it, and I sicked it straight back up into my bowl, and she *made* me eat it again!"

We gasped in horror. I hoped I would never have to go there. Not even for the luxury of having more food in front of me than I could eat would I have liked to put up with that!

Later a younger sister spent periods in a sanatorium at Standish, but unlike my siblings I never went. Sometimes I wonder if my passion for "soup" had anything to do with it. Because I had an abhorrence of cheese, then a staple part of working-class diet, I was allowed to put a saucepan on the hob for my "soups". All I needed was an onion and a bit of fat in any form such as a few bacon rinds, a nob of lard or dripping, or anything that would exude a bit of grease. I remember one evening I had an onion but there was not a scrap of fat in the house. Not even Granny next door could oblige.

"Tell you what, me wench, there's probably a bit o' grease in me washin' up rag. Thee'st better boil thic up wi' thee onion."

I might have done, too, if she had not stopped me.

Mother was advised by the doctor to give my little brother plenty of fresh scalded milk. Fresh milk was a bit of a luxury then, and we used to have cheap tins of skimmed condensed milk. Also this was very sweet so we saved on sugar as well. Mother gave me a penny to get some milk at Watson's Farm, a half-mile walk through the woods. It was a lovely day but I was full of trepidation about this errand even though it was for my little brother's sake. Please, please I begged the fates, don't let there be any cattle in the field I've got to walk through. I was only nine, and I had once been chased by a bull, and all cattle that had no udders were bulls to my mind. Luckily the field was empty and I ran through it to the farmhouse.

Rosie, one of the daughters, answered my knock, a fresh-faced English rosebud of a young woman. While she went off to fill the can I felt refreshed just looking into the spartan clean whitewashed back-kitchen. She filled the pint tin can to the brim for the penny and gave me a sweet smile and a few kind words to go with it. On the way home I had to walk very carefully not to spill the precious milk, and as I passed the sheer beauty of my surroundings suddenly overwhelmed me.

Under the majestic oaks tall foxgloves in their purple pink myriads grew among the thick green fern fronds and the hot sun filtered through the branches, like a benediction. The patches of springy soft moss, the twittering birds, the bushy-tailed red squirrels in their lightning forays among the branches — where had all this loveliness come from? This incredible earth, that teacher had told us was going round and round in space? And me. What was I? Who and why was I? The whole business was so richly fascinating and puzzling; full of questions with no one to answer; no one to thank for this sweet serenity in a forest glade. I could not cope with my emotions and I started to cry.

"I should think you've took your time," grumbled Mam, but I could see she was pleased with the full can of milk.

Old-fashioned country cottages with old-fashioned country cottage gardens and old-fashioned country cottagers to live in them are becoming just a memory, beautifully evoked in Flora Thompson's lovely book *Larkrise to Candleford*. That bulldozer, Progress, has destroyed them, and I feel privileged that in my lifetime I share memories similar to hers.

These days I would think more than twice before I dropped in on our friends without an invitation. They could be absorbed watching a favourite TV programme. When we acquired a car I felt no such inhibition as we decided to call on a pair of aged friends who lived in a cottage off the beaten track in the Forest. They would probably be busy right enough, but in tasks that could be put aside for friendship. We had to park the car and walk the narrow woodland track to the cottage, back through the sort of forest of my childhood, before housing estates, factories and access roads for cars and lorries had diminished its wildlife areas, back through time to that land of birds and little wild creatures, wild flowers, and more human effort to survive.

I knew when I got there that if I wanted to pay a penny I would have to go to the bucket privy halfway down the garden — a garden devoted to growing vegetables with a run for a few chickens, and some old-fashioned flowers for beauty and for the bees in the two hives at the far end. Nobody was about, the porch door was open and as we entered a voice called, "Come on in."

The old pair were sitting each side of a big black-leaded grate, and it was a joy to see their faces light up at the sight of us. The old woman moved the kettle on the hob over the fire to brew us a cup of tea.

"We be havin' a bit of a squat. 'Tis a bit o' work an' a lot o' rest for we two these days I be afeared," said the old man with an air of regret.

He was temporarily at loggerheads with his beloved old pipe. "Dattling thing! I packed the 'baccy in the varmint as careful as a bird buildin' 'is nestle but the bugger won't draw no how." He refilled it, and then taking a partly glowing cinder from the fire with his bare hand, a hand calloused and hardened by years of labour in the pit and above ground, he relit the pipe. This time it worked and he sat back puffing contentedly. A cup of tea was soon on the table, and I gave her a bag with a few goodies I had baked.

"Oh, there was no need for you to bring these, my wench; we've always got plenty o' victuals in the pantry these days."

"Aye," commented the old man, "that's one thing that 'ave improved from the old days. Not that I 'ad it so bad as some. My feyther was a real artful poacher, an' it weren't just fer rabbits neither. 'Im didn't leave all the pheasants to the gentry. Mother couldn't afford much in the way o' cheese to put in our sandwiches to take to the pit, but Feyther made sure there was summat to put between our bread. A lot wasn't so lucky. I remember one poor bugger workin' wi' a few on us on a coal seam, an' come bait time 'e'd go and sit away on 'is own, so one day I went an' sat by 'im, an' all that poor chap 'ad in 'is butty tin was a piece o' dry bread. 'Im was as thin as a beanstick, an' I knowed 'im 'ad a brood o' young 'uns at 'ome. I told Mother an' 'er give me a couple o' extra sandwiches. Next day I made out as I didn't want all me victuals an' give 'em to this chap. Well, 'im ate the one, an' then 'im put t'other in 'is tin to take 'ome. No, in that respect I bain't sorry to see them times gone."

"How's your son these days?" I asked them.

"Oh 'im an' 'is wife do live in one o' those grand 'ouses in a new estate over Cheltenham way, an' as fer as I be concerned they be welcome to it," the old man answered. "We was there to stay wi' 'em fer a few days a bit back, an' to tell the truth I was glad to come 'ome.

126

Mind you, they made us welcome right enough, but the place makes me feel like a fish out o' wayter."

"Yes, but it's very convenient," interposed his wife.

"Oh aye, 'tis a right box o' conveniences. A switch fer this an' a switch fer that an' a switch to kip you warm; not a sign of a fireplace, nowhere to draw yer chair up to when you've finished yer victuals, carpet everywhere so you be very near feared to go out in case you gets a bit o' dirt on your shoes. An' as for the garden they don't grow so much as a 'tater, just pocket-'ankerchiefs o' grass an' goin' to a shop to pay through the nose fer bedding plants every year. Then they sit by thic picture-box in the corner to fiddle the time away. An' come the week-end, they jump in the car to get away from it all.

"That grandson of ours do 'ardly know what 'is legs be for. 'Im do take the car to go to the post box a couple o' 'undred yards away, an' 'im do carry one o' they transistor radios about all the time. I dunno 'ow they young 'uns can listen to that pop music all the time. I don't think they do ever hear the birds a-singin' or the wind blowin' in the trees. An 'ims reckoned to be a clever scholar wi' 'is sharp talk about computers, but 'im don't know a brussel sprout plant from a cauliflower. It took millions o' years to turn monkeys into men, an' I reckon in a million years' time human beings'll be more like tadpoles, great big 'eads stuffed wi' a heap o' knowledge that's no use to 'em, an' 'ardly any legs.

"An' now them social service people do come worryin' the missus an' me to go into one o' they old folks' council bungalows! 'Twould be like puttin' a workin' dog into a satin-lined peke's basket."

He took a deep puff at his pipe, and got a nasty bout of bronchial coughing aggravated by the silicosis from his mining days.

Three cups of tea later and I had to walk down the garden to the bucket privy. It was obvious that the old couple were fighting a losing battle with the weeds rampaging between the vegetables. The door of the little stone outbuilding that contained the wash-copper was open. A neat pile of wood was out ready to light the fire under the copper. What a pity they had not got the electricity, I thought. Luckily the mains water had been laid on, and they no longer needed to draw heavy buckets from the well which was covered with a sturdy wooden lid. There was no curious grunting pig in the sty at the bottom of the garden. A sawing-horse was in there and some fallen limbs put ready that the old man had dragged in from the surrounding forest.

As I stood out in the garden the old man came out; he gave a few low whistles and his tame robin flew down to take a biscuit crumb out of his outstretched fingers. He must be eighty now, I thought, and his wife not far behind. I cursed old Father Time for destroying this country idyll, and making it such a cruel struggle for the old pair to carry on.

"Come again, come as soon as you can manage it," they said as they stood, bent and fragile, waving us out of sight. We never saw them again. With the minimum of fuss, first he then she took to their beds. The Social Security sent the district nurse and a home help, but they did not need their services long and they died within a fortnight of each other.

128

The cottage was sold. Now it has been enlarged and modernised out of recognition. The black-leaded iron gate has gone to the scrapyard, and a tank of central heating oil is in the place of the double lilac tree. The fowls' cots, the beehives, the rows of vegetables are now an area of sweeping lawns. The old couple would not want to return to their lost paradise.

Most of our phone calls are from our children. "I'm ringing to see if you and Dad will spend the day with us on Sunday," is a frequent suggestion from our Chris. He and his wife and young daughter then lived six miles away in the village of Redmarley.

Forty odd years ago I would not have shown my face in Redmarley. It was there I broke the commandment "Thou shalt not steal", but I do plead extenuating circumstances. At that time we were renting a share of a house in a field the other side of Gloucester Docks. The war had been on for nearly three years, and our Chris was eighteen months old. Syd worked in a local sawmill, and life in general, like the food rationing, was very stringent. One fine Saturday in late July my mother and my eighteen-year-old sister came for the weekend. Reading the local paper Mother noticed an advert for blackcurrant pickers on a fruit farm at a place called Redmarley, the pickers to get threepence a pound for their labours.

"I'll mind Chris if you two would like to go," offered Mother, adding that we could earn ourselves a bit of very welcome money and no doubt buy some blackcurrants cheap as well. We knew in which direction Redmarley lay; it would be a good way to spend a Sunday, and we would be able to get a bus there from Gloucester. We were up and ready bright and early. With Mother and Syd to cope with Chris I had no qualms about leaving him. Fresh fruit was scarce and precious. I had some jam jars and some Graham Farish tops, and I could already visualise them filled and on the pantry shelf — vitamin C for Chris in the long periods we never saw an orange!

The morning promised a fine day. Chatting happily we hardly noticed the mile and a half walk over the fields to the warehouses and docks, then across the river and into Gloucester to the bus stop at the western edge of the city. We were disappointed that it would cut down our picking time, but not unduly alarmed to discover that the bus to Redmarley would not come for another three and half hours. Oh well, we had long legs; we would walk it!

Although we were on the main road the walk was pleasant, with wide grass verges, hedgerowed gardens and farmlands, and only a sprinkling of houses. The sun came out, cheering and benign at first and then beating down fiercely on our hatless heads. After a couple of miles my sister began to limp.

"Ooh, I think I've rubbed a blister on my heel." She had. In wartime, stockings were far too scarce and precious to wear for blackcurrant picking; the edge of her shoe had rubbed the skin off the back of her ankle.

"Sit down a minute," I said and I scoured the hedgerow for some dock leaves which I wrapped round her foot.

At the next house an old man was leaning over the

gate. "Are we on the right road to Redmarley, and is it far now?" I asked him.

"Yes, you be on the right road, an' yes it be far, but you kip followin' your noses an' you'll get there," and just before we were out of earshot he added "zometime".

"Let's think of all the girls' names beginning with a," I suggested. Anne, Avril, Amy, Amanda: we carried on through the alphabet to Zoe and Zara. Then the boys from Alfred to Zachary. Surely by now Redmarley should be on our horizon.

"Could you please tell me how far it is to Redmarley?" I asked a woman who was hanging out some washing.

"Well, I dunno how far it be exactly, but 'tis a fair distance. Be you two walkin' it? Better you than me!" and she laughed and went in for some more washing. We picked more dock leaves to replace those that had disintergrated round the blister, and struggled on despondently. The thought of the blackcurrants was still enough inspiration to boost our aching legs. We drank a drop of our wartime ersatz lemonade; thirst had become another of our problems as the day had become a real scorcher.

"Don't let's ask how far it is again until we've passed three black and white houses," I suggested. These Tudor specimens only peppered the roadside at distant intervals, and just now they seemed to have almost petered out altogether. We passed by two more when my sister remembered something her teacher had told her.

"It was about some war in Greece, and this man had to run twenty-six miles to take a message from Marathon to

Athens. Well, he just managed it and then he dropped dead!"

"That's just what I'll do any minute," I groaned.

"Well, if you do, here's a chap coming along to bury you!" she said.

A tall gentleman wearing a clerical collar was approaching; surely he would bring us good news?

"Please could you tell us how much further it is to Redmarley?"

He was a very precise sort of person, and he started to give us precise instructions. Yes, it was about another four miles, perhaps a little more; After a mile we would come to three elm trees on the right-hand side of the road. Then we were to carry on up a gentle slope, then past some barns, and further on, a bungalow — but it was all too much for me. I dissolved into hysterics and collapsed on to the verge. I could not help it, I could not stop laughing. He looked a bit perturbed, and my red-faced sister was none too pleased either.

"I reckon he thought you were having a fit!"

"I was," I said, staggering to my feet. "It's the thought, you see," I gasped, "how the devil are we going to get back home!"

A man was standing by the three elm trees, so I thought I would find out how far we had come, for a change.

"Could you tell us please how far Gloucester is from here?"

"'Bout six miles as the crow flies, and about eight miles roun' the road." The information about the crows was not much use to us, but I worked out that tacking on

132

the one and a half we had done to reach Gloucester we had now walked nine and a half miles. Another three did not seem so bad now.

"When we get there we can rest our legs by picking the low branches sitting down." I was picturing the bushes loaded with bunches of luxurious ripe fruit.

At last, at long last, we came to the outskirts of Redmarley and got directed to the entrance to the fruit farm. Just inside the gate a woman sat with a trestle table with a pair of scales and chip baskets for the pickers. But where were the pickers? We could spot less than half a dozen wandering about on the huge field.

"Fill your baskets and bring 'em back to me. You can pick anywhere," the woman told us. Normally the pickers are allocated to rows.

When we started we soon found out why we could pick anywhere; the bushes had been picked clean. As we looked for fruit we parted to shouting distance of each other. After a long interval she called, "How many have you picked?"

"Half a mo', I'll count 'em; seven!" I shouted back.

We traipsed up and down and across, eventually getting to the top of the field where four other disconsolate pickers stood. Between us my sister and I had gleaned barely a pound of fruit.

"Well I don't know about you lot, but I reckon we've earned these buggers," grumbled a very fat woman. "They shouldn't have advertised for pickers so late. Why, we've earned about sixpence and I walked four miles from Newent to get here and wore out more'n six penn'orth o' shoe leather doing it."

"We walked from the other side of Gloucester and we've got to get back there somehow," I told her.

"Bloody shame I call it, wearing ourselves out on a fool's errand. I tell you what I'm going to do. I'm going to get through that gap in the hedge and take these blackcurrants with me. We can get on the road to Newent without passing where we came in." She looked at her watch. "If you two want to come, and you step it out a bit sharp, you'll catch the bus that goes to Gloucester from Newent this evening."

Like giggling, guilty children running from an orchard raid we followed her through the hedge gap. Incredibly fast for one of her bulk she led the way, the cheeks of her enormous behind swaying rhythmically from side to side. After about a mile we stopped for a breather near where the road branched off, and I put some more leaves round our blisters, for now I had some too.

"That road leads to Pauntley Court where Dick Whittington was born, and he walked the hundred miles to London, and I'll bet that poor bugger had some blisters on his feet," commented our stout friend.

When we finally reached home Chris was tucked up in his cot and fast asleep, while Mother waited full of anticipation for her currant-picking daughters. With our feet soaking in bowls of warm water we recounted our tale of woe.

Mother offered us a crumb of comfort: "Well, you did get nice and brown from the sun!"

"Yes, Mum, thoroughly browned off we are!" I agreed.

* * *

134

These days we drive the few miles to Redmarley, through leafy lanes intersected by Newent, and over a little ford where the River Leadon sometimes rises over the bridge. It is always a fresh pleasure to drive into the little village with its beautiful Tudor cottages near the old church. Here one must drive with care for in the middle of the road lies old Wally the basset hound. He is the self-appointed Squire of Redmarley, the guardian of the village, keeping an eye on all the visitors. If we emerge later on for a walk he will escort us far enough to make sure we are harmless before waddling back to his post.

Chris and his wife and daughter lived in one of a pair of tiny red-bricked cottages, unprepossessing outside, but inside as welcoming as a grandmother's warm lap. The huge oak beams in the low ceiling look ready to crumble at a touch, but the woodworm has retreated long ago from trying to penetrate their iron-hard interior. "Welcome," the cosy rooms seem to say. Generations have had shelter here, and these old walls have absorbed the sounds of many families in their joys and sorrows. And they are thick and sturdy enough to absorb them for many years yet.

The hands of its humble builders show in its bumps and crevices, hands that were proud to make a home with the simple tools and materials available. The old hearth warms your knees, the walls keep you sheltered, and if a few draughts come around the door it is only God's fresh air. Old cottages have character, they say, and how I agree.

Redmarley has spread out a little with some inevitable

modern housing, but the surrounding rich red land that named it is still used for agriculture on a large scale, and still produces some fine crops of blackcurrants.

Sometimes our outings were a sort of duty. A little bit of fame goes a long way. All sorts of women's groups asked me to speak at their meetings. Perhaps the fact that someone with my background and a minimum of education had achieved a little literary success made me a bit of a novelty. I felt completely inadequate for the compliment and would have liked to refuse, but publishers do not like shrinking violets. They invest money in what you have written, and expect you to do this sort of thing. A letter inviting me to speak to a group of ladies at the Speech House did bring me out in a bit of a sweat.

The Speech House is a fine ancient stone building in the heart of the beautiful Forest of Dean. A royal hunting-lodge in Elizabethan times when wild deer and boar abounded, it became a law court where twelve verderers sat in judgement on local disputes. Now it is also a hotel and conference centre. Once, when a young woman, I had gone there to be interviewed for a housemaid's job, but I was too overwhelmed by its grandeur to accept it. Once a year it did cater for the proletariat, allowing the annual fair to take place in the adjoining meadow. It was there, at the age of eleven, I got a salutary lesson in economics.

Riches are relative; a vagrant beggar searching at the kerb for fag-ends feels the same elation when he finds a cigarette packet mistakenly discarded with a whole fag

136

in it as Paul Getty did when he closed a deal netting him another million pounds. I felt as rich as either when one of my aunties came home for her holiday from domestic service and gave my a shiny sixpenny piece, "all for yourself to spend how you like." With hindsight I appreciate her generosity even more, for her wages were five shillings a week and she had a large family of sisters and a brother to share her precious savings. Her wages were hard-earned; she was a second housemaid for a grand family. As was often the case the mistress did not deal with the hassle of the servant problem but left it in the capable hands of the housekeeper, and the one at Auntie's place was a proper termagant. Auntie brought home her written list of duties. From her emergence at half-past six from the attic bedroom she shared, until her duties were over in the evening, her list of jobs accounted for every minute of the day except meal-breaks.

Granny could not read, but Grancher could, so he read it out to her and commented drily to Auntie, "An' what if thee behind do get an itch? They a'n't even allowed thee time to scratch theeself."

I was wondering how best to spend my windfall, when an exciting idea came into my head. Next Saturday was Speech House Fair day. We had been told that Speech House had once been a royal hunting lodge where Queen Elizabeth had once slept. If that lady had really slept in all the places rumoured, the warming pans must have been in constant use airing her royal beds.

Fact or fiction I could not say but I *did* know that the Fair was coming to the grounds of the Speech House. I was eleven years old, but to go there on my own seemed an awfully big adventure. Had I been cast in the same mould as my generous Auntie I would have shared my sixpence with my best friend Gladys and taken her for company. Alas I was not, and anyway had not Auntie said "all for yourself"? But now I was wealthy, who among the village girls was affluent enough to come with me? There was only one possibility, a doubtful one, Evie.

No one played with Evie very much, and I did only occasionally; "a spoilt little wench" was the general verdict of the villagers. She had been born late to her parents when her two brothers had already started work in the pit, and they all adored and indulged her. She also had a childless uncle and aunt in the village, and they petted and spoiled her. It was nothing for her to be given a whole penny to spend, but she wouldn't give you a lick of a sweet, nor the core of her apple to finish off. She would run off in the middle of a game of hopscotch or houses in an unprovoked sulk and not speak to one for days — a remarkable feat, I thought, for though I could sulk a bit myself I was too mouthy a chatterbox to hold out for long. So I felt a grudging admiration for her will-power, and I found her character a challenge.

To my surprise, when I broached the idea of coming to the Fair she agreed, and she was ready when I called for her on the Saturday morning, and even richer than I with sevenpence in her pocket. As we started off on our two mile walk I felt some trepidation in case she might suddenly turn on her heel and decide to go back home. She hardly spoke, but that was no matter; it was so pleasant walking through the woods. In those days children wandered the Forest without fear. There had never been cause to warn us of speaking to strangers. If we passed an unknown man in the Forest he would probably greet us with "Hello, my little wenches", and then ignore us. We passed the slag-heap from Trafalgar pit, the slag-heap where a young man we knew had been killed by a fall as he worked in it trying to pick out bits of usable coal; this practice was against the law but a great temptation for those out of work with no miner's allowance of coal.

But sad thoughts did not linger long. Joyous anticipation was whetted as our long walk brought us within the sound of the fairground music and the hum of the crowds. Soon we could see the field turned into a magic carpet of roundabouts and swings, fairground games, coconut shies and side shows.

We began by just looking at this feast of novelties, and my attention was soon caught by a man who was inviting people to throw a penny on to a metal table festooned with small squares. For every penny that landed in a square without touching the lines he would give a prize of sixpence.

The incredible wealth of my sixpence had already diminished a little as I looked at the amount of tempting delights to spend it on. A go on the roundabouts for a penny; twopence a go on a spinning wheel with an arrow that stopped on a number. If the number was on your ticket you could choose from a wonderful array of prizes; twopence for a ride on the swingboats; a bag of highly coloured sweets for a penny; the list seemed endless. Surely I thought, I could throw a penny to land in the middle of one of those squares! It looked simple enough. The man saw my interest and obligingly changed my sixpence for six pennies.

The first one that I threw did not land true, and he whipped it off with speed of a chameleon's tongue. Disappointed, I threw another. Another failure, I could hardly believe it. Three more goes as desperation crept in. Now I was down to my last penny; surely, surely, I could not possibly miss this time. Oh, how thankful I would now be to get my sixpence back! I threw again, and again I missed. I stood there penniless. There was not a glimmer of sympathy from the man, who had now completely lost interest in me and was busy cajoling others to follow my foolish path.

Whilst I had been seeking my fortune Evie had bought herself an ice-cream cornet. The pangs of hunger and thirst were now hitting me. The two pieces of toast and dripping I had eaten for breakfast seemed a whole world away. My parched tongue nearly hung out as I watched hers licking the delicious cool yellow ice cream. "I've lost all my money on that game," I said piteously, but she was as uninterested as the man on the stall. I was mortified by my idiocy and full of grudging envious admiration of her commonsense. She bought herself another cornet. I tried to distract myself by looking around, but with an empty pocket and a gnawing hunger all I longed for was to go home. But it was my idea to come here, so I trailed along beside her and wallowed in my misery as she bought some humbugs, and then gulped down a penny glass of pop.

"Come in, come in. See the Human Mermaid," a fairground man was shouting, "only one penny to see this remarkable sight." I was taken aback when Evie paid out twopence and gave me a shove to go in with her.

Inside, in a small roped enclosure, a young girl lay on a shawl-covered mattress. She was a very thin, pathetic, fair-haired creature in a soiled white sleeveless dress that revealed four fleshy stumps instead of arms and feet. Her sad eyes tried to avoid the eyes of the onlookers. My heart ached for her helplessness, and the old saying that you can always find somebody worse off than yourself struck home and true. This poor girl could not even get up and run away from the indignity, nor even wave an angry hand at her tormentors. And she never would be able to, never. As far as I was concerned Evie's uncharacteristic generosity had been misplaced. I took a leaf out of her book and was too churlish to thank her.

What a relief when at last she made her way to the exit gate and we headed for home. Every now and then as we walked along she would put another humbug into her mouth. My pride nearly came to breaking point to try my luck and ask for one, but I held out until we reached a point a mile from home, where a woodland turning led to the Forest Keeper's Lodge. Keeper Lee's wife was a regular chapel-goer; she had a plump friendly face and kind brown eyes. I decided to knock at her door and ask for a cup of water. Evie followed me. At first my knock at the back door appeared to bring no response, and just as my heart sank down into my boots the door was opened by Mrs Lee.

"Please could you give us a drink of water, Mrs Lee. We've got very thirsty walking through the woods."

"You just sit down on that bench a minute, my dears."

And back she came; not with a cup of water, but with two brimming mugs of milk and a plate with two pieces of currant cake on it. Non-chapel-goers, often with cause, decried the holier-than-thou attenders as hypocrites, but Mrs Lee seemed like an angel's messenger to me, and her refreshment manna from heaven. Now I had plenty of stamina for the last mile home.

Dad was there, sitting by the table after the evening meal. "Your Mam is next door in Granny's," he said. "'Er 'ave left your tea and your share of the rice pudding on the table."

As I ate it I poured out my tale of woe. Dad listened attentively but gave me precious little sympathy. "Well, you know that old sayin', my wench, that money is the root of all evil. Now you 'ave learned that it's the misuse o' money that's the cause o' so much misery. You was tryin' to do it but you was up against a' expert. Now suppose all your pennies had won you sixpence each, an' thic man 'ad lost all that money, maybe 'im 'ad a lot o' young 'uns at 'ome an' they could a' gone short thanks to the like o' you. Folks as do want summat for nothin' by makin' big profits is nothin' but robbers, an' thic man on the stall was exploitin' that side o' 'uman nature, an' there's plenty o' that sort about. That's what economics is about, my wench, an' that's why 'eaps o' people be goin' short while the smart alecs have got a lot more than their share."

My day that had started off like a rocket was ending

like a damp squib. But the experience did not destroy the germ of avarice firmly planted in my psyche. I still find it hard to resist a "bargain".

CHAPTER
THIRTEEN

It was nice to go visiting friends but even nicer when our favourite friends came to visit us. Top of the list were Flo and Pat, and Pat's sister Ciss who had become as dear as another sister to us. Ciss came quite often to stay for weekends, sometimes with Flo. Now and again Pat, Flo and Ciss would come down from London for the day by train. From the age of seventeen to forty, save for my few despairing dashes in the war, I had lived in London, and often got bouts of homesickness for that grand old capital. Just listening to their London accents and expressions helped to assuage the ache and oh! how we could chatter about the experiences shared through the years, and our children. What a lift it gave to my spirits to see any of them walk down our garden path!

Then came the day when Flo told us that she had found a small lump in her breast and it had been diagnosed as malignant. She was quite calm. Ciss had already had a mastectomy some three years earlier and appeared to have quite got over it. Flo was going to be admitted to hospital in a few days time. When I put my mind to it I can prepare some really nice meals. It was a relief to see Flo and Ciss tucking into everything, though I was perturbed by Flo's swollen ankles, and Syd and I both felt down-hearted as we waved goodbye to them at Gloucester station; and the next couple of years were to be the blackest in my life.

We were relieved when Flo phoned from the hospital to say she was having her mastectomy in two days time. But the relief turned to great distress when Ciss phoned the next day and told us Flo had had a stroke, and was being sent home to recuperate from it. There would be radiation for the cancer instead of a mastectomy. Dear Flo! She struggled through the stroke, and Ciss went with her for the radiation and then chemotherapy treatment.

Because of a broken engagement when he was a young man, Ciss's brother Charlie had remained a bachelor and had lived with Ciss and their mother since the war. Their mother had died recently at the age of ninety. Charlie and Ciss were both heavy smokers. The terrible cough he developed forced him to go to the doctor, and a hospital diagnosis revealed incurable cancer of the lungs, Charlie put his affairs in order, continued to play golf, went on a holiday to Spain, and never complained or bemoaned his fate. He kept his spirit unbroken until the last few days before his death. During this time he and Ciss often stayed with us and his calmness and courage made me feel very humble. He was sixty-eight when he passed away, the same age as my own brother Charlie.

When my brother was sixty-eight, and had smoked heavily all his life, he too developed a terrible cough. His wife persuaded him to see a doctor. The first X-ray at the hospital revealed nothing significant, but in a matter of weeks he was rushed in for an emergency operation. He was a dying man, riddled with cancer. To see him daily deteriorating over the next few weeks was unspeakably dreadful! How I felt for Flo and Ciss and Pat!

Ciss had been so occupied looking after her brother, being a great support to Flo, and doing a little part-time job to boost her old age pension that she had given no thought to her own health. The lump that was developing in her remaining breast she put down to a muscle strain. Until she began to feel an awful nausea and weakness. She went to the doctor but it was too late; she had a cancer and it had spread to an inoperable degree. The chemotherapy made her feel even worse. She was glad to go into a hospice for the little time she had left. I felt a hopeless sense of outrage at Nature's cruelty.

"Why, oh why?" my spirit screamed into the unknown. But there was no response. The one ray of consolation was that Flo seemed to be winning the fight against her cancer. Soon after Ciss's death, Flo went for her check-up at the hospital. The growth was gone; the radiation and chemotherapy had beaten it! The sense of relief when our phone rang with the news was indescribable!

"We'll come down and see you soon, and we'll bring a bottle of champagne!"

Pat had made his way in the world, and they were comfortably off. It was only a few weeks to Christmas. "I'm booking up a few days over Christmas in a nice hotel in Bournemouth as a treat for Flo; no work or cooking for her this Christmas" Pat told us. So all was well. So we thought. But only three weeks later Pat phoned to tell us Flo was back in hospital. I could hardly bear to think about it. The cancer had spread into her bones. Pat took her home, and the wonderful Macmillan nurses came in daily. My spirit is haunted by the picture of that lovely woman when we went to London to see her twelve days before she died. A gentle beautiful wraith of her former self, the misery of her existence was becoming too great for her to bear. She too was ready to spend her last few days in a hospice.

I was plunged for the second time into the melancholia I had experienced when my father was killed in the pit. I have never found a cure but the balm to make it bearable came from our children and grandchildren and the few close friends that are left. What magical and enchanting creatures grandchildren are, especially when they are very young, and family love and the simple pleasures are all to them. It takes a long lifetime to realise that these two aspects of living are the most important. So we old ones and they little ones are on level terms and get on famously together. They are the heralds that carry our genes to a brief and tenuous posterity before Nature by cross-breeding fades us out.

Keeping busy is also a helpful factor in combatting grief, especially if it brings a challenge, and one came along directly. I was surprised, no, astonished, when a letter came from Pat Truman, director of the Swan Theatre in Worcester saying she wanted to produce a play from my first book *A Child in the Forest*. And she wanted me to cooperate with actor David Goodland in writing the dialogue. This was new territory for David and for me. He knew a great deal about the theatre and I knew practically nothing, but I am an obstinate old woman, and I had known intimately all the "characters" in the play. We argued our way through many an afternoon with give and take on both sides, and I now regard him as a very nice young friend. Eventually we got a script together, and now it was up to Pat Truman.

I was full of doubts and trepidation, with not enough nerve to go to the opening night. It was scheduled to run for two weeks. I knew that Pat Truman and the cast, which included David Goodland, had given of their best. I never saw a rehearsal; it was too far for us to go. Chris and his wife and Jenny and her husband went to the first night while Syd and I minded the baby, our tenth grandchild. They came home very impressed and full of praise for everyone concerned. It had been a packed house and two curtain calls. It ran to full houses for two weeks, and an extra Saturday matinée was put on as well. Syd and I still full of doubts went to a mid-week matinée where I was recognised, to some acclaim. Flo's recently widowed husband Pat came down to stay with us so that he could come too. The theatre was packed to capacity. I had not been to a theatre for thirty-four years, and only twice before that, so I was no judge, especially of something so close to me. The whole experience was utterly bewildering like some sort of dream. The acting was superb, Pat Truman had done her job well, and more than once I saw a tear run down Syd's cheek at too clear

148

a memory. Myself I was too numbed by the strangeness of the whole experience. I did not feel like myself at all.

When the play was put on again, three years later, at the Everyman theatre Cheltenham, for three weeks, I was more prepared for the experience. It was a somewhat different interpretation, this time by Sheila Mander. She too had got a wonderful response. This time we did go to the first night. Flanked by the family and some of the grandchildren we were ensconced in the front row of the circle. The theatre was filled to capacity, and our Jenny whispering in my ear "we're all so proud of you, Mum" helped me to bear the nostalgia that the play evoked. Sadly our brother-in-law had followed his beloved Flo to the grave a few months previously, but it was good to see his eldest son Leslie and his wife there from London. So many fellow-passengers on the same train of time as us had reached their earthly destination, leaving so many, too many, empty places for the rest of our journey.

CHAPTER
FOURTEEN

Getting involved with my past again probably brought on a vivid dream about the time when I worked as a fourteen-year old maid-of-all work to a nonagenarian lady in the Cotswolds. The exciting thought occurred to me that we had a car now, and I could actually go and visit after almost fifty years. I started my cajoling tactics on Syd, and by Sunday I had got him in the mood to humour me. The twenty-mile drive to Stroud through the Gloucestershire countryside was a pleasure but the couple of miles from Stroud to the village had changed a good deal from when I had walked it all those years ago on the old lady's errands. New houses, building and garages had sprung up on the roadside.

Syd stopped the car by what used to be a pin factory beside a delightful little canal, and we began the steep uphill walk to the cottage. I must be a masochist; as my old legs ached with the effort I began to weep inside for my tireless-legged fourteen-year-old self. A sharp curve in the road revealed the stone wall of the cottage's back garden. Much of it had collapsed, and the stones had been removed. The back of the cottage looked much the same, but the picture I had carried in my mind's eye crumbled to dust.

The cottage must have been unoccupied for years. Not a stone remained of the old wall that surrounded the front garden. The old tall creaking wooden gate, and the laurels that flanked it, were gone, and what had been an enchanting country garden of fruit trees, flowers and neat rows of vegetables was just an area of couch grass peppered with dandelions. There was no trace of the little narrow lawn in front of the door set off with three standard roses, nor of the wooden seat to which the old lady had hobbled on her stick, to make sure I whacked the dust out of the mats.

The cottage had evidently been bought and was in the throes of being modernised. I felt sick and shocked. I looked up at the window of the bedroom where the old lady had insisted that I slept with her to keep her company in the big four-poster bed. It had been a year of bondage tied to whims and demands, but the beautiful setting and the views across the valley had more than compensated for the clipping of my young wings.

Here I had my fifteenth birthday, and that had been a red-letter day in my life. On that morning I had received my first-ever birthday cards; two of them. One from a beloved old village neighbour and one from a school friend in service in Cheltenham. They were shiny postcards illustrated with flowers, the most beautiful and exciting presents I had ever had. I kept them handy to keep on peeping at them. It was no reflection on my family that I had had none from them; our poverty had been too great to acknowledge birthdays by cards or otherwise, and it had never occurred to me to send one to anybody. That made this surprise all the more delicious.

In the afternoon I had been in the garden pulling a lettuce for tea when the creak of the garden gate made me look up, and there coming through it was my elder sister. It couldn't be, oh, it couldn't be, I thought as I ran to greet her.

"'Ere you be; summat for thee birthday." She handed me a box. In it were three dainty handkerchiefs packed in the shape of flowers, exquisite squares of coloured lawn, far too lovely ever to be used on my snub nose.

The cost of them and of the fare to visit me made this a most generous gesture for my sister. At five shillings a week I was getting a shilling more than she. She too worked as a maid-of-all-work for a very impoverished maiden lady. She had started at five shillings a week, after a time reduced to four and six, and now to four shillings. But my sister stayed there, mainly to suit herself. She was a composition of talents never to have a chance to flower. An exceptionally beautiful girl, she could paint and sew, embroider and upholster, she could sing like a lark and was highly intelligent, and a squarer peg for the round hole of domestic drudgery could hardly be found. But she was a manipulator of people too and had built a relationship with her employer that suited her well, by gradually bringing her talents to her notice.

"Bless you, I do spend hours on me arse mendin' 'er clothes, an' workin' flowers on 'er tablecloths, an' I do paint the woodwork in the house, an' suchlike, while 'er

152

do get on wi' the washin'-up an' the dustin'. I do hate dustin'!"

I was a bit nervous of how my tart old mistress would take the idea of having a visitor, but as it was my birthday she allowed my sister to sit in the kitchen with me and have some tea. The cups of tea, and the bread and butter and cake, went down very well.

"Gawd, I was famished," said my sister. "Well, I be famished most o' the time. 'Tis all swank and victuals where I be. Her do use damask tablecloths, silver serviette rings, bone china, an' 'ardly anything to eat. D'you know, she buys the cheapest streaky bacon for breakfast, cooks a bit every mornin' an' fries a bit o' bread in the fat. One mornin' she 'as the bacon an' me the bread, an' the next mornin' the other way about. 'Er do cut off the bacon rinds to add a bit o' flavour to them penny packets o' Maggi's soups for our dinner. Mind you, I do 'ave a good blow-out once a fortnight, when Frank do come! Him do bring fish 'n' chips for us."

Frank was my sister's fiancé: by our standards an affluent young man, learning the building trade, and the possessor of a motorbike. Once a fortnight he drove out to see her.

"And do 'er let Frank visit you?" I asked; kitchen callers for maids was not the done thing.

My sister chuckled. "'Er don't know anything about it. When 'im's comin' I do start on 'er after our Maggi's soup. 'You don't look at all well, Miss Weekes,' I do say all sympathetic like. Poor old dear, 'er do like a bit o' fuss. Long 'afor Frank do come I 'ave got 'er up to bed

153

thinkin' 'er's 'alf dead. And o' course," she said with a wink, "we do keep very quiet!"

It was a terrible wrench to wave her goodbye. If I had not had the cards and the handkerchiefs to gloat over I would have thought it was all a dream.

CHAPTER
FIFTEEN

"I'm going to Cheltenham tomorrow, Mummy," announced Jenny. "Cavendish House have started their sale. Would you like to come with me?"

She could not realise how her casual air impressed me. The very name Cheltenham and Cavendish House evoke in me the flavour of apartheid as I remember the period when I worked there as a young domestic servant. In those days it seemed to me that Cheltenham had two social classes, mistresses and maids, and only people with the money and the social standing of servant employers entered the portals of Cavendish House. Without the influx of modern-day traffic and the garages that serve it, and without the infiltration of some cubist architecture amongst its Georgian splendours, Cheltenham was then a much more gracious, quiet and beautiful town. But this did not compensate for my deprived existence there. I had landed myself, in servant's idiom, with a "starve-guts" job.

Anyone with social pretensions in Cheltenham kept a maid, and with wages at about five shillings a week they mostly got a bargain. In my case I had the entire cleaning of a narrow three-storey house plus the washing, and the afternoon care of a toddler and a baby, taking them for their fresh-air walks. And all this with very little fuel in the way of food.

To preserve the look of the façade the window of the narrow boxroom at the front matched that of the main bedroom. But this boxroom, which was my bedroom, had only space for an iron army bedstead with a couple of army blankets for cover, and some hooks behind the door to hang my clothes. There was not even space enough for a chair. Just the same it was a haven where I could forget the pangs of hunger, and fall into exhausted slumber under the rough army blankets.

One summer night when I had the window wide open I did not wake up during a heavy thunderstorm. When the alarm clock woke me at six my bed was soaked up to my chin where the lashing rains had beaten in. I reported this matter to my mistress, but she ignored it, giving me no change of bedding nor any means of drying mine. I reckon that bed was still damp when I left the job. Perhaps that started off the arthritis that plagues my old bones now.

One afternoon a week, and every other Sunday, I was free from two pm till ten pm. There were many girls from our village working in service in Cheltenham. I was friendly with one of them, Jane, and she had the same time off as I. Halcyon hours they were. Taking care that we did not rub shoulders with "our betters", we too could stroll down the promenade; we too could look wistfully at the window display of Cavendish House, or meander through the lovely richly-flowered public gardens. The gateaux and the other fancy cakes in the Cadena Café made our mouths water, but we had neither the money nor the courage to join the élite inside at the tables. But a sweet shop was no obstacle. With a bag of chewy toffees each we spent our last three hours in the cinema, and went home to our beds to hug our pillows and dream we were Vilma Banky or Janet Gaynor in the arms of Rod La Rocque or Charles Farrell.

As Jenny and I walked through Cheltenham I fell to wondering what had happened to Jane. I would not recognize her now. She was a bit older than me and must be an old woman of seventy or more now. But she has always been one of the conundrums among my close acquaintances. When we were children Jane was one of the nicest girls in our village: a gentle refined type who somehow never got as mucky and untidy as the rest of us in our games, nor spoke with such a Forest dialect of thees and thous. She did well at school and was much too kind and sweet-natured to be scorned by the rest of us for her ladylike ways.

She went into service as second kitchenmaid in one of the residential preparatory schools for boys which abounded in Cheltenham. Nobody was surprised when she was quickly promoted to head parlourmaid. When she came home for her holidays there were plenty of young miners in our village anxious to walk out with her.

However Jane had caught the attention of the young postman who delivered to the school where she worked. A sensible steady pair, they scrimped and saved for nearly four years to start their married life in a well-furnished cottage they rented on the outskirts of the town. There was plenty of work for daily cleaners, and

Jane-like she worked all her spare time until they could risk putting their savings down to buy their own little house in a working-class area. She continued to fit in going to work, when, at two-year intervals, their two baby boys were born.

Nobody was surprised how Jane had got on; our village was quite proud of her. Then came the war. Women took over postmen's duties, and Jane's husband was called up. He was sent to Japan and taken prisoner. The Americans came to Cheltenham: GIs with plenty of money in their pockets, and nylons and chocolate.

Some time later an incredible rumour reached the ears of our village: Jane had been seen in the company of GI soldiers in a public house, made up like a dog's dinner and the worse for drink. Never! Never, was the shocked response; not even the most avid gossip would believe it or repeat it. It must have been someone who looked like Jane! But the rumour persisted.

About a year later Jane staggered off the bus at our village stop; she was already in the first pangs of labour as she got to her widowed mother's door. The shocked mother took her up to bed, panicked enough to call in a neighbour, and sent for the doctor. It was a putrid birth; Jane's company among the soldiers had seen to that. The baby girl, blind and deformed, was a travesty of Nature.

"As God's my witness, the doctor was hoppin' mad. 'You dirty little bitch!' 'im called Jane. I was there an' I 'eard 'im say it". The village reeled from the blow and felt profound sympathy with her mother.

Jane took her little crippled baby home, and everybody conjectured what her husband would say when, if ever, he came home. It was a two-year wait. In the meantime it was ascertained that Jane was a most devoted and caring mother to the infant and to her boys, whom a neighbour had looked after during the birth. There were no more pubs for Jane and no more keeping company with soldiers.

Her husband returned. Perhaps his life in the army and his incarceration as a prisoner of war had taught him great compassion. He stayed with her and together they picked up the pieces of their ravaged marriage.

I did not see Jane for some years. Heartbroken after the funeral of my father I was in a bus going back to London. Jane had been visiting her elderly ailing mother. Shabbily dressed but looking neat and groomed, she put her arms around me. "I be sorry to hear your bad news." She was again the kind and refined Jane that I had known, but when I think of it, her uncharacteristic lapse still blows my mind.

CHAPTER
SIXTEEN

I suppose that in autobiographical literature I have obtained a smudge of fame. It came late in my life with its blessings and its drawbacks. But just sixty years ago, at the age of seventeen, I poked my plebeian snub nose through a door which could have led to fame in a different media — the films. "A likely story", anyone would scoff as they look at me now!

Often it is the people at the bottom of the heap who indulge in the grandest day-dreams. Like most seventeen-year-old girls at the time, I was film-struck. A precious four pence out of my weekly wage of ten shillings was spent on "Picturegoer" and "Film Weekly". In my dreams I changed my identity every few days and became Nancy Carroll, Constance Bennett, Sylvia Sidney, although I always drew the line at Gloria Swanson; even my imagination would not stretch that far! Nor did I ever visualise actually going on the films, nor really ever wanted to. These day-dreams were just a vicarious escape from the everlasting scrubbing, polishing, window cleaning, washing-up and laundering — drudgery that was my lot every day of every week.

I did not have the gumption to ask my Jewish employers in London's Aldgate for a weekly half-day off. It was Becky, the eleven-year-old late afterthought in that large family, who became a remote substitute for the little sisters I could see only on my annual holiday, and it was she, my little friend who sometimes got me time off to go to the pictures. "Tell me, Winnie, if there's a picture you want to see, and I'll tell Mummy I want to see it. She won't let me go on my own so I'll say I want you to take me." So we went. These outings whetted my appetite for day-dreaming, but I had practically no chance to read my film magazines.

At night I shared a room with Becky. We would lie there and play "I spy", or have a gamble, each backing a bug to crawl up to the ceiling first. But very soon I would fall into exhausted slumber, and all too soon early morning came again and another full day of domestic labour.

My fifty-six year old mistress could not read or write. She had come here as a peasant girl from Poland, and had hardly known shoes to her feet. She was driven out in the purges of 1911. She had found work in a sweat-shop tailoring factory in the East End, and had been glad to marry a fellow-worker. He was a Jewish widower and had five children, and she bore him another five. One of the sons, with the business acumen and determination common to his race, started a furrier's business from scratch.

The business prospered and he now employed almost the whole family and a couple of cousins and a brother-in-law.

Now it was 1931, and I was seventeen, and I had just come back from my two weeks holiday at home in the

Forest. My heart was aching unbearably at the conditions my family were struggling in. The miner's strike in the Forest had been over a long time, but there was still no work for Dad, a wise, kindly, articulate man who had started work in the pit at the age of eleven, self-taught to appreciate the works of Darwin, Einstein, and Marx; and books such as Erewhon, Tess of the D'Urbervilles, Pickwick, The Ragged Trousered Philanthropists. His conscience and the injustice of his mates' conditions had made him a gifted orator. But the pit-owners victimised him for his opinions, and for seven years he could get no work, only a meagre day here or there wherever a man was wanted who would do any kind of labouring for next to nothing. Our village neighbours who were in work lived in abject poverty, but in spite of this a bucket of coal appeared now and then by our back gate, or a bit of dripping in a basin, or an anonymous two-shilling piece in an envelope. They tried to help, but my Dad and Mam seemed to have shrunk, and my two little sisters and brother were obviously and seriously undernourished.

No longer able to spend a few coppers on the comfort of a bit of baccy for Dad, Mam dried wild colts-foot leaves in the oven for his pipe. But it was a poor substitute and forced him out into the woods to retch. On a stomach so empty he could not even be sick. In their letters they had not let on how desperate things were. I had sent a half-crown postal order from my wages now and again; now I determined to send every penny I could manage. I told Becky I was saving up and would not be taking my two film magazines. Dear Becky! She spent twopence of her own pocket money on a "Picturegoer" for me.

Every Thursday evening, in readiness for the Jewish Sabbath which was Friday to Saturday, I cleaned the family silver and brass on the big kitchen table. It was mostly heavy ornate candlesticks and the best cutlery. I spread newspaper over the table and put my "Picturegoer" underneath. When my mistress dozed off, or was busy cooking in the scullery, I read my magazine. This ploy I learned from the youngest son, Nat, who used to put his comic under the pages of the Talmud which he had to study every evening. Then one evening I read an article in my "Picturegoer" about making films at Elstree and how the "extras" got a guinea a day!

A guinea a day for taking part in crowd scenes! No need to be able to act! It was a fortune! I could work six days a week. For six guineas I could get digs, live comfortably, and send more than half home to Mam. That would be more than Dad would get in the pit, even if he was taken on again. Oh, what a fool, what an idiot I was, not to have found this out sooner! No silver candlesticks ever got such an enthusiastic polishing. Now I must write to Elstree for a job at once.

The article said that the studio was owned by British Dominion Pictures, but gave no Elstree address. However I found their Wardour Street address elsewhere in the magazine, and that night in bed I wrote my letter. I explained that I was seventeen and an avid movie fan, that I had had no acting training, and did not want to be an actress, but I would love above everything to earn my living as a film extra. I would not mind what hours I worked, or what I had to wear, or what I looked like. I had noticed in film features how the measurements of the stars were always emphasised; perhaps extras had to send theirs too. So I took mine:- bust thirty-seven, waist twenty, hips thirty-seven, height five feet six. I had one photo, shoulder length with a beret perched on the side of my head, so I enclosed that as well. I was ignorant of the significance of my pulchritude, although I do not expect a modern seventeen-year-old miss to believe me. My tiny waist was in part an inheritance from my pocket-Venus mother, and was emphasised by the habit of my poverty-stricken childhood of keeping something permanently tied there to keep up the odd assortment of underwear I had covering my nether end!

Sure enough a few days later a long pale-green envelope arrived addressed to me; I took it into the toilet to read it. It was from a Mr. Fred Daniels, the photographer who did the stills for the studio. The letter came from Elstree, but it also bore the address of his studio in Coventry. It requested that he would like to see me at Elstree within the next two weeks. My hopes and excitement were almost more than I could keep to myself. Now I had the courage to ask for, and would have demanded, a long overdue half-day off. Rather taken aback, my mistress conceded, first working out which day the following week I could best be spared. Luckily it was summer-time. I had a "best" dress; a pale-blue crêpe, a "reduced bargain" off one of my mistress's daughters. My only make-up was a dab of Pond's vanishing cream on my snub nose. But I did not think my looks would matter, and I had a poor opinion of my round plebeian face anyway.

I took a train to Elstree, and then found I had quite a walk; but no matter, this prolonged my excitement and my curious anticipation. The studios looked like a long, low and very large factory. A commissionaire stood guard in a little building at the entrance to a huge courtyard. He looked at me in a very doubtful manner when I told him I had an appointment with Fred Daniels. Finally he picked up a 'phone to confirm this, and another commissionaire came across the courtyard and escorted me to the studio waiting-room, and told me to wait. On a round polished table a beautifully produced portfolio of the stars employed by the studios caught my attention. Just sitting there in a room where they might have sat seemed an incredible achievement. I turned the pages:- Gracie Fields, Anna Neagle, Madeleine Carrol, Chilli Bouchier, Tom Walls, Robertson Hare . . .

My absorption was interrupted by a short, pleasant looking man in his forties who introduced himself as Fred Daniels.

"And you are the young lady who wants to be a film extra?"

"Yes, please."

"All right. Now let me see you walk across this room."

With the benefit of hindsight I can imagine what he saw in this seventeen-year-old girl walking across the room in her figure-clinging blue crêpe dress.

"Now, would you like to come round with me and see a little of the studios?"

"Oh, I'd love to."

Large rooms opened off wide corridors which were stacked at the side with all sorts of props. A large empty set showed three sides of the interior of a country mansion drawing-room, with stairs leading up to nowhere; a "set" for the popular films made with Tom Walls and Ralph Lynn and Winifred Shotter.

My guide explained about camera angles and lighting while I listened avidly, too interested for any shyness, and ready to comment. We went back to the waiting-room, and he asked me what I did for a living. I told him, although my swollen rough housework hands had probably told him already. After some apparent thought he said "I'm afraid 'extra' work would be no good for you. It is so unpredictable; maybe three or four months at a time with no work. And you would have to register with an agency, and pay them commission on your earnings."

My spirits sank to zero, but he went on, "However, you seem to be a very intelligent girl, and you have a lovely figure. I think it quite possible you could get a contract to do 'bit' parts. That would mean regular money and much higher pay than an 'extra'. And besides, I don't think you should mix with some of the types who go in for 'extra' work. Of course, the producers would want some photographs of you. Could you come next week for me to take some?"

"How much would they cost?"

"Oh, nothing. But I don't keep my equipment here. I have rooms in Elstree at 14 Oak Way. My landlady is Mrs. White. Will you come there next week?" And he told me how to get there; I was not likely to forget. This was all too marvellous, but I had better delay a fortnight, for asking for another half-day so soon was beyond my courage.

Mrs. White herself answered my hesitant knock on her front door. She was a pleasant middle-aged woman in a flowered pinafore, and she showed me to a door on the first floor. Fred Daniels answered my tap, and we sat down in a large room, part of which was curtained off into a kind of alcove. There was a camera on a tripod, and two or three hand cameras in a corner of the room. After a little chat to put me at my ease (which did not work), he showed me inside the curtained alcove. It contained a full-length mirror, a bench and a stand for hanging clothes. On one end of the bench was a Hussar's braid-trimmed officer's coat, tasselled hat, and a pair of high-heeled shoes.

"Slip your dress and petticoat off, and put these things on while I set up my camera. Come out when you are ready." Behind the curtain I did as he instructed, and I thought I looked a weird sight in the mirror. The coat was too big, the shorts too short, the high-heeled shoes a bit tight, and the hat had to balance somehow on my head. I stepped out. He did not laugh, as I had thought he would, but got me to pose on a chair with my legs crossed at a sideways angle to the camera and a lot of my legs showing. Then I had to turn my face to him. He adjusted the hat to a jaunty angle then told me to put on an expression as though I had caught someone doing something mischievous. He took several shots and then told me I could dress.

Greatly relieved I did so, and then he took my face from several angles. The session was over.

"Could I come next week?" Emboldened by my progress I agreed.

The next week's session went rather differently. This time Mrs. White brought up tea and biscuits when I got there. When she had taken the tray away he showed me the photographs. I could hardly believe that the girl in the Hussar's outfit was me. I looked like a saucy chorus-girl, and quite a pretty one after his artful touching-up of my face. The other pictures showed my face in favourable and unfavourable angles. He said that a producer was interested but wanted some photos of a more glamorous kind. All that was in the curtained alcove this time was a large piece of satin brocade. Casually he said, "Just take off all your top clothes and drape this around you leaving your shoulders bare."

Satin brocade is slippery stuff to handle. I had quite a job fixing it so I could hold it together just showing my bare shoulders. At last I stepped out and sat on a chair in front of him. "Come on, you can show a little more than that", he laughed. He started to adjust the drape himself. It fell off, and before I could grab it back I was briefly a modern page three girl. My terrible embarrassment was heightened when he bent down and gently kissed the exposed curves. Tears sprang to my eyes. I felt that this was a sort of rape. I did not know this man. I did not love this man. There was a hurt inside me that I could not explain.

Looking back I blame my naïve stupidity more than him. Actually he was very patient and explained that such inhibitions were not indulged in by film actresses. Only the previous week he had taken some lovely nude pictures of Chilli Bouchier on a stretch of beach very early in the morning. But her husband had come with her. This sort of thing was all normal in the films. I was now completely out of my depth. I had seen Chilli Bouchier in a film; she had seemed quite a normal sort of young woman.

"We'll see how these turn out, anyway. Then you come again next week. Come on, I'll drive you to the station this evening." He kept his car, a luxurious low open-top model, in a garage nearby. I could not help feeling grand when in front of a garage-hand he came round and opened the door for me to step in. When we got to the station he looked at his watch. There would be a train in five minutes. Then to my further bewilderment he put his arms around me, and boldly gave me the kiss of a practised lover. My healthy physical seventeen-year-old body could not stop the sweet response to that kiss, but my spirit rebelled. An instinct of self-preservation was also aroused. What a dilemma I had got myself into!

Utterly dejected, the train journey was Hell. On the one hand my family were desperate, but my Dad and Mam would break their hearts if I let a man take photographs of me with nothing on, and I could not face the idea anyway. Then the remembrance of my two little sisters and brother, with their pinched faces, pot-bellies, and stick-thin legs came to haunt me. I was in torment.

A couple of days passed during which I got some

scoldings for being absent-minded. And then I got a letter from home.

During my holidays I had been to see where a new mine was being sunk in the woods about half a mile from the village. A new house for the new manager of the new pit was being built and was nearly finished. It brought no hope or joy to my parents. Still blacklisted by the mine-owners, there would be no job for Dad at this pit. However, in desperation, he had asked for a job clearing up the builders' rubble and laying out the garden for the new house. He had been taken on by the wife of the new young manager when she came to inspect her domain. Later he was introduced to her husband, a liberal-minded independent young man who had obvious sympathy for the miners' grievances. And he had told Dad that by the time the garden was laid out there would be a job for him in the new pit.

My relief and joy at reading this news were so wonderful that I had a job not to take the liberty of hugging my mistress. Little Becky had already gone to school. That bedtime I wrote another letter to Elstree apologizing to Fred Daniels and thanking him for his efforts on my behalf, and offering to pay off in instalments any expenses I had incurred. But I had now changed my mind, and I did now want to work in films in any capacity.

I received a very nice reply, including two pounds fee for my "modelling", and a promise to write to me again from Cap d'Antibes where he was accompanying a film unit. He wrote again, twice. I did not answer. I was a grateful escapee from an unknown world that I no longer wished to enter.

CHAPTER
SEVENTEEN

We feel lucky that three of our four children live in country cottages in beautiful Gloucestershire; Nick, the youngest son, lives in the Cotswolds. As we drive directly on the main road the thirty-eight miles to visit him and his family, we pass many delightful and tempting by-ways. But there is ample compensation at the journey's end for we have come to their village in the heart of one of Gloucestershire's loveliest estates. Not one garish poster or red brick mars the tranquillity of the Cotswold stone. Take away the traffic from the road, and the television aerials from the houses, and one could forget the industrial revolution completely.

Almost always there are admiring visitors strolling through the village and peeping over the immaculate drystone walls at the well-kept lawns and flower beds that front the noble Stanway House. It dominates but by no means diminishes the charms of its little church by the gatehouse, the famous ancient tithe barn behind the churchyard or the group of old stone cottages on the other side of the road, their footings perpetually washed by a clear and tinkling stream embanked with primroses, and each front door approached over its own little bridge.

On summer Sundays the tenants play their cricket nearby, their pavilion a thatched structure with a long seat elevated from the damp earth by saddle stones. Wives and children shelter from the heat beneath walnut and pear trees, and prepare tea for the players. Old men in faded straw hats, clenching their pipes in unsafe dentures, mutter about the heroes of the past. Rustic England at its best.

Nearby, in a triangle of cut grass, stands a fine tree, its stout old trunk decorated all round with a wooden seat to tempt the visitors to rest their legs. Here is another pair of delightful cottages and an ancient building that houses inside it an enormous water wheel. What medieval engine or pump or grindstone its rotten oaken paddles drove, no one can say. Behind, and blending into the landscape as if it grew there, is a sawmill shed with piles of stacked timber where the sawyers can sit in their mealtimes and gaze at the gently-sloping meadows dotted with trees and sheep and a gnarled old apple orchard. The little stream that once drove the great wheel rushes unhindered down the dark mill race and out into the sunlight to meander merrily through the valley with patches of watercress for those in the know.

Every summer, to raise money for charity, the gardens and part of the Big House are opened to the public. Then the magnificent old stone-tiled tithe barn supported by crutch frames becomes an Aladdin's cave of beauty and colour for the flower arrangers' and gardeners' competitions. The vegetables displayed on long trestle tables are a credit to the fertile soil and to the gardening lore handed down through the generations. No doubt the lectures at the Womens' Institute have put a polish on the talents of the flower arrangers. On our visit, every adult entry seemed worthy of an artist's brush and canvas. If the children's wild-flower efforts were less imaginative, how lucky they are to be able to pick them on their own doorsteps!

Syd nudged me. "Oh look, here's some children's prize tickets with our name on." We had been rather steered in that direction by a little granddaughter. We paid our due of admiration, and then joined the other two in the gardens. Grandad bought the ice creams and I bought the raffle tickets from our daughter-in-law's prize stall. The girls ran off to watch some young ballet dancers on the lawn, and Syd and I paid our fee to go into the Big House.

And big it certainly is; too big, I thought, to be a home. Freedom of thought — if not expressed thought — is everyone's prerogative, and my thoughts as I walked around were that the famous Chinese Room, with its ugly but priceless furniture, day-beds and decor was as tasteless as the gaudy vases on many a cottage mantlepiece. But there were things of great beauty and interest, and a sort of ancient shove-penny table, just an enormous plank, its incredible length cut surely from a Brobdingnagian oak! I envied the occupants their library, and there was a sitting room which endeared me to its users. It contained some priceless china, a couple of lumpy armchairs no better than some I had seen dumped on bomb-sites in poor quarters of London, a pot-flower in a plastic container on a priceless antique table, and some beloved child's crude drawings hung on the walls. Here in the pomp of this grand house humanity flourished strongly.

Phew! What a rambling place to keep clean! What a millstone of responsibility around one's neck, I thought, with a sense of relief that it was not mine.

During its long history it had once been a summer residence for the Abbot of Tewkesbury. Again I pondered how far Christ's disciples had strayed from the humble path He trod, and from His advice to resist the temptation of riches on earth. What a hedonist this ecclesiastic must have been! The contrast between the Big Houses and the tiny cottages of the tenants is evidence of two traits in the human spirit — greed and the servility to accept it; a loss of dignity to both sides. The Abbot holidayed in Stanway House! Our son Nicholas, a carpenter as Christ was, and living in this enormous area of rolling fields and pastures, cannot afford a pony for his horse-mad eldest daughter!

Nowadays, abbots have been trimmed down to size, and the homes and status of the tenants greatly improved. And as Nick remarked, the beauty all around is just as enjoyable seen through his cottage windows as through those of the Manor. His cottage is a gem with a large garden and a small stone barn converted into a workshop. They live in a little earthly paradise, and after the fête we went back to it for a slap-up tea.

We sat back replete and relaxed, but not for long. Becky, eight years old, our youngest granddaughter, had plans for us.

"Come on, you two," she said, "I'll take you for a walk." Taking our hands in hers she led us out to their big lawn. Here under the apple tree we had to give their fat, woolly pet lamb a hug. They had cared for this orphan for a farmer who had no time for it, starting it off with bottle feeding. I remember the look of shocked horror on my daughter-in-law Elizabeth's face when I asked if it was destined for their freezer.

Then we had to peep at an abandoned baby hare the girls had found. Nick had made a run and a hutch for it. "We'll let it free as soon as it's big enough." We were taken to admire Becky's strutting bantam hens in their coloured feathers and then we were led off up the hill and into the woods.

"I'll show you my fairy tree. It's all hollow in the middle. I put a biscuit up there for the fairies, and there are fairies, Nanna, 'cos when I come to look the next day the biscuit is always gone."

What a secret and wonderful world a thick wood is! As we picked our way up the wide and rutted path Becky suddenly branched off into the undergrowth in places taller than her little person. "Come on, follow me, you'll be all right," called our intrepid little guide.

Still distinguishable among the weeds were the stone edges of some mediaeval path that led to the tumble-down remains of a tiny dwelling. Its window-space revealed a small dark room with a grateless hearthstone, and its stone-tiled roof was still strong enough to support a dead tree fallen across it in some wild storm. What manner of long dead hermit or peasant could have lived there?

"Daddy said that a long time ago this was the house of

a monk," announced our Becky proudly, oblivious of the gloomy sadness all around.

Further along the path she took us down a side-track to a gentle moss-covered dip. "This is our Dingley Dell where my friend and I come for picnics. It's a secret, but you two can know. And down in the meadow just over there," she pointed vaguely, "there's some gigantic blackberry bushes. When you come over later on, Nan, I'll help you pick some for your freezer. There's millions of 'em, great big juicy ones. You have to jump over a stream to get there, but I can do it so I expect you could if you tried hard, and there might be some watercress for you to take home. Now we're going to my fairy tree.

At last we came to her *pièce de résistance* the fairy tree, the hollowed trunk of a huge, dead elm. "There you are," she said, "the biscuit's gone again. And my cups and saucers I put for them last year are still there." Her cups and saucers were acorn shells, tiny ones standing in bigger ones.

"Do you like my fairy tree, Nanna?"

Oh Becky, Becky, I love your fairy tree. I love the world you inhabit. I long to discard my tired old self and live in your little frame. You are *me*, Becky, me as I was those long years ago when I believed in fairies, and when I too was a child in a forest!

I know I do ramble on about the charms of the country cottages but I am also aware that they do have their drawbacks, a point that needs no emphasising for one of our London friends. James is a bachelor with a brilliant intellect. Having not lumbered himself with a wife and family he has been able to indulge in the search of knowledge on many subjects abstruse or practical.

We knew that our rusty-cated brains were in for a bit of an oiling when he wrote to say he would like to visit us. We had then been in our tied cottage for a couple of years. He is a considerate chap; knowing of our primitive conditions with four children, he booked himself accommodation at a modest hotel seven miles away in the heart of the Forest. He is also a keep-fit fanatic, and though middle-aged he chose to walk through the woods and across the fields to get to us. It was an ideal September day. Syd was at work and the children at school. Not knowing what time he would arrive I prepared him a cold meat and salad lunch.

Our steep hill made even him out of puff and he thankfully sank down at the kitchen table for a cup of tea. "Don't bother to lay my lunch up in the other room. I'll eat here in the kitchen and keep you company," he offered.

Our kitchen was fairly small, and over the table which was against the wall I had got Syd to put me up a cupboard. Thinking that James might like some of my homemade blackcurrant jam to go on his spare bread and butter I leaned over him to reach an opened pot from the cupboard. As I did so he obligingly went to get up out of my way and gave his forehead a sharp knock on a corner of the cupboard and hit the jam pot out of my hand. The jam had not set too well and the contents cascaded over his beautifully laundered shirt. The shock made him jump up again, this time giving himself an even harder bang against the cupboard. In panic I began to slosh him down with bowls of cold water. He looked quite shaken and decided to escape from me and my cupboard through the back door and out into the garden.

There was no time to warn him. Because of the way the roof sloped down at the back this door was very low. We had all got used to ducking down. Poor James! He really bashed his cranium and fell on the steps that led up to the garden, steps made very earthy by our muddy wellingtons. It took him all afternoon sitting in our courtyard to recover.

However after his evening meal in the sitting room with Syd and the family he waxed loquacious again. When he left late in the evening we had been brought up to date with current affairs, some of the strange ways of microscopic organisms, and the theological aspects of Tibetan monks. He had acquired some extra knowledge too on his noble cranium; he had learned to be wary of old cottage doorways.

All those years ago when James first visited us I was in my early forties, and if the need arose I too could walk seven miles. Now when I feel in the mood to defy the advancing years it stretches my legs to the limit to walk the couple of miles to our Jenny's cottage near the summit of May Hill. This is a pleasant enough walk from where we live now, but not to be compared with the one when we lived much nearer, in the tied house. Then the walk was an enchanted mile.

One of Gloucestershire's landmarks is the group of trees on the top of May Hill. Like the gaze of the Mona Lisa, wherever you are within a radius of many miles, those trees seem to be keeping an eye on you. Until several decades ago, the peak of May Hill, exposed to all the elements and the winter gales, had proved too bleak to grow a tree. Then the newly-resident Squire of the local Manor who was a keen arboriculturist made a wager that he would plant trees there that would survive. He imported some very hardy seed from Canada, and eventually he won his wager and left this unique feature on the Gloucestershire landscape. His son inherited the estate and the father's love of trees, and he reforested many acres of his land.

It was to one of this gentleman's tied cottages on the lower slopes of May Hill that we moved thirty-seven years ago. It was summertime, and the first Sunday we could spare the time we walked up to the top of the hill. After the crowded streets of Marylebone we felt that we had indeed come to the land of milk and honey.

Pollen-laden bees buzzed past us as we climbed the path through the cherry orchards. Then on we went through a meadow of tall lush grass, buttercups and clover, where a swathe had been cut for a footpath. On our left a dense wood, cool, dark and mysterious, decorated a steep bank and disappeared out of sight into an undergrowth of bracken, brambles and ivy which made ideal cover for the young pheasants we glimpsed. In the middle of the meadow the broken sails of a tall windmill hung forlorn and useless — a rusting skeleton, once an abortive attempt by the Squire to bring piped water to some of his tenants' cottages. Here we stood and turned to look back at the wonderful view and down on to the roof and dormers of our own cottage folded in on its little plateau, and we felt like royal inheritors of this pastoral kingdom. At least Syd and I did; the boys were eyeing the windmill, no doubt with the idea of climbing it when parents were not about.

We were equally enchanted with what we could see on the slopes ahead — little meadows and orchards, tiny meandering lanes, the hillside dotted with cottages and gardens planted in true cottager's style — the sort of gardens where a migrant seedling is allowed to grow in its own sweet and inconvenient way because of its beauty. Fowls scratched and tethered goats munched away on little areas of common land. Here and there a notice, "new laid eggs", or "honey for sale", tempted me down paths edged with pansies, candytuft and old-fashioned pinks. Nearly every garden had its plum and apple trees, the branches laden with ripening fruit. A small church, a chapel and a village hall catered for the spiritual and social needs of the scattered community. The Sunday gardeners, bending their aching backs to fill buckets of weeds from their rows of vegetables, probably gave a quiet oath or two that these interlopers grew even better than their own crops in the fertile soil.

Nearer the summit the houses and gardens petered out into a grassy area, now National Trust: a favourite picnic spot for many climbers, good horse-riding country, and a place among the foreign trees to see the grandest view in Gloucestershire — large tracts of several counties, the Welsh mountains, the Malvern Hills, the Dean Forest, the Severn Vale with its great shining river winding its serpentine way into the mist of distance; and straight ahead, over Gloucester Cathedral, showed the noble Cotswold ridge.

In the autumn the steep lanes on the way down offer a bonus of blackberries, sloes and wild rosehips for the picking. On the side of one such lane not far from the summit our Jenny now lives with her husband and son in Honey Patch Cottage. It is an apt name, for the large garden is a paradise for bees. The previous tenant seems to have planted almost every species of flower and shrub that grows in an English garden. From the winter jasmine and the snowdrops right round to the Christmas hellebore, things are abloom at Honey Patch. The sloping contours of the garden, with its rockeries, little lawns, lily ponds, shrubberies, and flower-beds would make a land fit for Oberon and Titania to rule, and the hovering butterflies could be their messengers.

There may not be fairies at the bottom of their garden, although you might well believe it, but at the top of it there is a tiny wooden dwelling that looks as if it might have some elves. It does not. An old man lives there, his roots and way of life firmly anchored in the past. No television, no electric cables, in his home — a paraffin lamp and candles suffice for him. He does his washing in a copper with a fire beneath, heating rainwater caught in a butt. The whiteness of his fortnightly laundering of sheets, pillowcases, towels, and underwear puts my machine-washed efforts to shame.

He tends his own neat-hedged plot, and does some odd job gardening to augment his pension. In the matter of dress he simply ignores the seasons, never taking off his jacket in a heatwave, never donning a topcoat in the bitterest weather that winter can bring.

No one knows what it is like inside his little wooden house; no one is asked over the threshold. Not even Jenny — but he does allow her the privilege of baking him a weekly cake and tart and keeps his independence by leaving by her door some of his home-grown vegetables. Surprisingly he pays them the honour of his company on Christmas Day, perfectly content to sit away the day from ten in the morning until eleven at night, on a seat by the fire, with a good view of the television, and his meals served up at his side.

This is his one-day-a-year lapse in his programme of ignoring progress and the march of Time. But Time has not ignored him. Arthritis has bowed his legs and made him cut a walking stick from the woods, and bronchitis forces him to bother the doctor for cough mixture which Jenny collects for him.

One Sunday morning he knocked on the door at Honey Patch, and breathing very wheezily asked to be taken to the doctor's surgery. Despite Jenny's assurances he would not believe that the surgery would be shut on Sunday morning. So she got the car out and drove him the five miles to a closed surgery, and nobody about.

"That's funny," he wheezed hoarsely, "'twas open the last time I came on a Sunday. I remember it well 'cos I walked across the fields," he added in a piqued fashion.

"Well, when was that, then?" asked Jenny

He lifted the peak of his cap and scratched at his bit of grey hair to stir up recall. "Well, 'twas a bit ago, I'll allow. Oh, I do remember now. The war 'adn't been over long. Must've been nineteen forty-five or six, I 'spect."

When the bubble of laughter in her throat had subsided, Jenny promised to phone the doctor when they got back.

To live in the cherished habitat of May Hill, conscious that Nature is slowly squeezing the breath from one's body, must be a tough cross for a lonely old countryman to bear.

Serpents come into every Eden. As the old man sat listening to "The Archers" on his battery radio by the light of an oil lamp, for he had no electricity in his little two roomed wooden hut — two of them in the guise of young male louts entered his home; whilst one pinioned his arms behind his back, the other ransacked the humble interior until he found what remained of the old fellow's life savings, a little under two hundred pounds. They left him tied in his chair and cleared off without trace. Local sympathisers soon collected more than the stolen amount, but they could not heal his broken spirit; shaken and disillusioned they admitted him to hospital for a check — he never came out, he had lost the will to survive. For a handful of pound notes the villains had shortened his life and gravely burdened their own consciences for the rest of theirs.

I feel a lot of sympathy for today's youth, especially the underprivileged ones. They live in a world where the baser instincts of mankind are liberally catered for. Lust — pornography remorselessly pushed under their noses. Envy — the unemployed youth with no money for a bus

ride, watching the status symbol cars of the more affluent. Aggression and law breaking, plenty to whet their
appetite on TV programmes and the constant TV
features from the war zones of the world.

Immorality is encouraged by many famous people
flaunting their sexual deviations and excesses often for
fat fees in the press — not only the gutter press.

Sloth — unemployment means idle hands — advanced technology and science have taken the simple tools
of living out of many hands, driving men from the land
into factories and offices to invent and produce more
extraneous luxuries with which to pollute their environ-
ment. Religion is losing its credibility for modern
thinking — Man has been to the moon, he passed no
angels or Heaven on his journey. Yes, I have much pity
for the youth of today — but not enough to forgive the
heinous louts who robbed that old man.

CONCLUSION

The fire wants making up. I lift the lumps gently with the tongs so as not to disturb Syd who is asleep in the armchair the other side of the fireplace. It is almost fifty-six years since we met. I recall the six-foot tall, thin, undernourished twenty-year old, soon turned by my care and cooking into a well-built, fine, handsome specimen of manhood. Oh! the fits of jealousy I suffered from the open admiration he inspired in the female sex! He is still a handsome old man, but the years have taken their cruel toll. No longer can he enjoy the solace of his treasured pipe. A heart attack and a spell in intensive care three years ago put a stop to that. A year before that I too had given up smoking because of a couple of minor strokes. Giving up has undoubtedly prolonged our lives, but other problems make both of us frail and tired.

Just coping with living has kept me too busy most of the time to dwell on the imponderables. Now I have too much time for thinking. At the age of seventy-eight I feel as overwhelmed and puzzled by this experience called existence as I felt as a wonder-struck child in a forest glade seventy years ago. To What or Whom do I owe the ecstasies, heartbreaks and all the in-betweens of my life? Countless millions think that they have found the answer in a multiplicity of gods in the form of humans, animals, trees or the sun. Most believe that their god or gods will take them to a spiritual after-life that will last for ever, or a transmigration into an animal existence, or to a mythical heaven where they will be reincarnated in human form. In our ignorance we cannot be blamed for clutching at such straws to escape the unbearable thought of our own mortality. But this comfort is denied me.

In the Kingdom of Earth, man is undoubtedly cleverer and more advanced than any other form of life. In his conceit he thinks all other forms of life, animal, mineral, flora and fauna, are here for his benefit or aggravation. Man is genius and fool, god and devil combined, but not one has yet produced a satisfactory answer to the questions; "How was the Beginning" or "Why Creation should want to make the billions of mankind", and "all to what end." I close my eyes with the darkness of my thoughts. Even popes, bishops, ayatollahs, are glad to use man's medical skills to put off that Heaven that they preach about.

"Oh, come on. Wake up, darling. Here's a nice hot cup of tea. It's still snowing, but I've checked the plants in the shed and I've put the extra polythene over them in case of a bad frost. Have a look at these plants in this gardening book while you're drinking your tea. Shall we get some this spring?" I have borne Syd four children, and I have tried despite my faults to be a good wife, but one of my most satisfying achievements was getting him interested in gardening. The rest of the world can have its Rolls-Royces, luxury cruises, villas in Spain, fame and fortune, he feels not one jot of envy. To walk around our garden paths, especially in summer, to drink in the beauty of the flower borders, to survey the rows of fresh vegetables and the neatly edged lawns, all the result of our own labours, and the chance to stand and stare in between the hoeing and the weeding, this is Syd's idea of Heaven and it's on this Earth! I pray that Nature in whose power the remainder of our lives undoubtedly rests, will grant us a few more seasons together in our garden.

ISIS publish a wide range of books in large print, from fiction to biography. A full list of titles is available free of charge from the address below. Alternatively, contact your local library for details of their collection of ISIS large print books.

Details of ISIS complete and unabridged audio books are also available.

Any suggestions for books you would like to see in large print or audio are always welcome.

7 Centremead
Osney Mead
Oxford OX2 0ES
(01865) 250333

ISIS REMINISCENCE SERIES

The ISIS Reminiscence Series has been developed with the older reader in mind. Well-loved in their own right, these titles have been chosen for their memory-evoking content.

FRED ARCHER
The Cuckoo Pen
The Distant Scene
The Village Doctor

BRENDA BULLOCK
A Pocket With A Hole

WILLIAM COOPER
From Early Life

KATHLEEN DAYUS
All My Days
The Best of Times
Her People

DENIS FARRIER
Country Vet

WINIFRED FOLEY
Back to the Forest
No Pipe Dreams for Father

PEGGY GRAYSON
Buttercup Jill

JACK HARGREAVES
The Old Country

ISIS REMINISCENCE SERIES

MOLLIE HARRIS
A Kind of Magic

ANGELA HEWINS
The Dillen

ELSPETH HUXLEY
Gallipot Eyes

LESLEY LEWIS
The Private Life Of A Country House

JOAN MANT
All Muck, No Medals

BRIAN P. MARTIN
Tales of the Old Countrymen
Tales of Time and Tide

VICTORIA MASSEY
One Child's War

JOHN MOORE
Portrait of Elmbury

PHYLLIS NICHOLSON
Country Bouquet

GILDA O'NEILL
Pull No More Bines

VALERIE PORTER
Tales of the Old Country Vets
Tales of the Old Woodlanders

ISIS REMINISCENCE SERIES

BIOGRAPHY & AUTOBIOGRAPHY

NINA BAWDEN
In My Own Time

SALLY BECKER
The Angel of Mostar

CHRISTABEL BIELENBERG
The Road Ahead

CAROLINE BLACKWOOD
The Last of the Duchess

ALAN BLOOM
Come You Here, Boy!

ADRIENNE BLUE
Martina Unauthorized

BARBARA CARTLAND
I Reach for the Stars

CATRINE CLAY
Princess to Queen

JILL KERR CONWAY
True North

DAVID DAY
The Bevin Boy

MARGARET DURRELL
Whatever Happened to Margo?

BIOGRAPHY & AUTOBIOGRAPHY

MONICA EDWARDS
The Unsought Farm
The Cats of Punchbowl Farm

CHRISTOPHER FALKUS
The Life and Times of Charles II

LADY FORTESCUE
Sunset House

EUGENIE FRASER
The Dvina Remains
The House By the Dvina

KIT FRASER
Toff Down Pit

KENNETH HARRIS
The Queen

DON HAWORTH
The Fred Dibnah Story

PAUL HEINEY
Pulling Punches
Second Crop

SARA HENDERSON
From Strength to Strength

PAUL JAMES
Princess Alexandra

BIOGRAPHY & AUTOBIOGRAPHY

EILEEN JONES
Neil Kinnock

JAMES LEITH
Ironing John

FLAVIA LENG
Daphne du Maurier

MARGARET LEWIS
Edith Pargeter: Ellis Peters

VICTORIA MASSEY
One Child's War

NORMAN MURSELL
Come Dawn, Come Dusk

MICHAEL NICHOLSON
Natasha's Story

LESLEY O'BRIEN
Mary MacKillop Unveiled

ADRIAN PLASS
The Sacred Diary of Adrian Plass Aged 37 ³/₄

CHRIS RYAN
The One That Got Away

J. OSWALD SANDERS
Enjoying Your Best Years

VERNON SCANNELL
Drums of Morning

BIOGRAPHY & AUTOBIOGRAPHY

STEPHANIE SLATER WITH PAT LANCASTER
Beyond Fear

DAVA SOBEL
Longitude

DOUGLAS SUTHERLAND
Against the Wind
Born Yesterday

ALICE TAYLOR
The Night Before Christmas

SOPHIE THURNHAM
Sophie's Journey

CHRISTOPHER WILSON
A Greater Love

GENERAL NON-FICTION

RICHARD, EARL OF BRADFORD
Stately Secrets

WILLIAM CASH
Educating William

CLIVE DUNN
Permission to Laugh

EMMA FORD
Countrywomen

LADY FORTESCUE
Sunset House

JOANNA GOLDSWORTHY
Mothers: Reflections by Daughters

PATRICIA GREEN, CHARLES COLLINGWOOD
& HEIDI NIKLAUS
The Book of The Archers

HELENE HANFF
Letter From New York

ANDREW & MARIA HUBERT
A Wartime Christmas

MARGARET HUMPHREYS
Empty Cradles

JAMES LEITH
Ironing John

LESLEY LEWIS
The Private Life Of A Country House

GENERAL NON-FICTION

Peter Marren & Mike Birkhead
Postcards From the Country

Desmond Morris
The Human Animal

Phyllis Nicholson
Country Bouquet

Frank Pearce
Heroes of the Fourth Service

Dava Sobel
Longitude

Sheila Stewart
Ramlin Rose

Joanna Trollope
Britannia's Daughters

Nicholas Witchell
The Loch Ness Story

ANIMALS

DAVID ATTENBOROUGH
Zoo Quest to Guyana

ALAN COREN
Animal Passions

MONICA EDWARDS
The Cats of Punchbowl Farm

PAUL HEINEY
Pulling Punches
Second Crop

PETER IRESON
Guiding Stars

SARAH KENNEDY
Terrible Pets

GLENDA SPOONER
For Love of Horses

ELISABETH SVENDSEN
Down Among the Donkeys
For the Love of Donkeys

ELIZABETH MARSHALL THOMAS
The Tribe of Tiger

GARDENS & PLANTS

DAVID ATTENBOROUGH
The Private Life of Plants

ALAN BLOOM
Come You Here, Boy!

RICHARD BRIERS
A Little Light Weeding

CHRISTOPHER LLOYD
In My Garden

JEAN STONE & LOUISE BRODIE
Tales of the Old Gardeners

TRAVEL, EXPLORATION & ADVENTURE

CLIVE ANDERSON
Clive Anderson: Our Man In . . .

DAVID ATTENBOROUGH
Zoo Quest to Guyana

PETER DAVIES
The Farms of Home

EDWARD ENFIELD
Downhill All the Way

KEATH FRASER
Worst Journeys: Volume One
Worst Journeys: Volume Two

JOANNA LUMLEY
Girl Friday

JOHN MCCARTHY & SANDI TOKSVIG
Island Race

PETER MARREN & MIKE BIRKHEAD
Postcards From the Country

DERVLA MURPHY
The Ukimwi Road

M. SCOTT PECK
In Search of Stones

CHRIS RYAN
The One That Got Away